GW01236669

CONTENTS

———◆———

CLAIMED BY THE KING

SHIFTERS OF BLACK ISLE #1

LORELEI MOONE

eXplicitTales

Copyright © 2018 Lorelei Moone,
Cover art by Silver Heart Publishing
Published by eXplicitTales
All rights reserved.
ISBN-13: 9781717731043

the Deep

Black
Isles

Siren's Rock

the Northern Sea

Hythe
Bay

White Cliff

the Post

West
Hythe

East
Hythe

Mainland

No Man's Range

CHAPTER ONE

———◆———

Once in every eight springs, a girl will be put forth by one of the coastal regions. A peace offering, a condition of the truce between the Giant Warriors of Black Isle and the men of the mainland.

1. No one shall remain with the offering when the time comes.

2. No one shall attempt to lay eyes on or follow the giants.

3. No girl shall ever come home, or her village shall feel the giants' wrath.

By this ritual we are bound, so long as our truce may last.

My life is over.

Kelly sat down with her head in her hands, making sure she could no longer see the eerily dancing shadows created by the candle on the kitchen table.

They never did waste much time between the lottery and the banishing.

Perhaps that's for the best, Kelly thought. *If I had a lot of time to think about this, perhaps I'd be less likely to cooperate.*

Of course, she still wasn't willing to accept her fate, no, she had other plans.

After dusk, she would be left on the shores of the Northern Sea, tied up to the strong wooden post erected solely for this purpose, until the giants claimed her.

Perhaps they wouldn't like her. Perhaps they'd leave her behind, demanding a prettier, daintier candidate? Kelly could only hope as much. Or perhaps her ties would be loose enough to wiggle free, allowing her to run before the giants even arrived.

Ever since her mother passed when she was only eight years old, she hadn't felt this alone in the world. Her father had betrayed her. He was meant to keep her safe, those were her mother's last words. *Keep Kelly and Ferris from harm, swear it to me.*

Instead, what had happened under the watchful eye of their father? She'd been chosen in the lottery.

It's an honor, he had said. *Your sacrifice ensures the safety of our people for the next eight summers.*

Kelly was to be made into a prisoner and slave, never to be seen again by her people, all of whom were just pleased none of their own daughters were chosen. She'd never gotten along with most of the villagers, most of whom took great pleasure in pointing out that her mother's death was God's punishment or other such nonsense. Kelly wasn't lady-like enough apparently. As a child she'd played with the boys out in the field rather than stayed at home and helped with the housework. If that was sinful enough to warrant her own mother's death, then she wanted nothing to do with such a God, or the feeble-minded people who believed in him. Of course, she could have never said that aloud, or they would have branded her a witch and punished her. So she had kept these thoughts to herself all these years.

And yet, she was chosen to protect those same people. Oh, the irony. She would love to see their faces when they realized that there'd be hell to pay for her upcoming escape. All those years playing with the boys would pay off. Now that she had reached a full eighteen years of age, Kelly wasn't half as weak as most girls she'd grown up with.

A horn blew in the distance, signaling that her wait was over.

It was time.

Her father opened the kitchen door, his weather beaten face tense - the only indication so far that he even cared what happened to her. *An honor*. What a joke.

He'd get over the loss of his first born daughter soon enough, at least he still had a son to focus on.

Ferris would miss her the most. Two years younger than she was, he'd always looked up to his big sister with admiration rather than the disdain others had shown her. She had been there for him more like a mother than a sibling, making sure there was food to eat, clothes to wear, even toys to play with.

Their father had never realized that he had been suffering the most after their mother had passed. While Father had stuck to his same old routine; heading off to the tavern after nightfall, as though nothing had ever changed, *she* had been there for Ferris.

Yes, Ferris would come looking for her as soon as he realized what had happened.

Father had conveniently sent him off on some merchant ship as a deckhand only weeks before the lottery. As if he'd known what would happen…

"Kelly. Our fate lies in your hands." Her father waved Kelly forward with an outstretched arm.

She hesitated for a moment, but took a deep breath and finally got up.

"Yes, Father."

Mother, I wish you were here. Kelly swallowed hard.

"Come in," Father called out.

A group of villagers made their way inside the cramped little kitchen. They surrounded Kelly, who had already assumed the position expected of her: her arms were crossed behind her back, ready to be tied. They wouldn't take any chances, because in the heat of panic, many an offering had attempted to flee in the past.

Oh, Mother. Why did you have to leave me to this fate?

Kelly's eyes stung uncomfortably, though she tried not to let it show. A cold gust of wind from outside dried her tears.

As soon as the rough ropes were tightened uncomfortably around her wrists, it was time to head towards the shore. A long procession had already formed outside Kelly's modest family home, which in this dimmed light looked like nothing more but a dilapidated shack.

Of the sun, already vanished behind the mountain

ranges towards the west, nothing remained but a reddish glow.

Fittingly gloomy, Kelly thought.

A few wisps of clouds did nothing to conceal the full moon shining down on Kelly's march towards her doom.

Towards the front of the procession two drummers would set the pace for everyone. Some of the villagers carried torches, deep shadows cast over their solemn faces, making it seem like they were wearing masks. These were not the features of the ordinary folk of West Hythe. Tonight, everything had changed. More change was yet to come.

Kelly lowered her head as she stepped forward, positioning herself between the butcher and the tanner, two of the strongest, and tallest men of her village. Their function was ceremonial as well as practical during this ritual: supposedly they'd ensure she was delivered to the right people, and not snatched by anyone on the way to the beach. Actually, it was more likely they were there to prevent her from bolting out of fear.

The drums started to roll, before settling into a comfortable marching pace, and the procession started to move. Kelly resisted for a split second, before being hauled forward by the butcher on her right.

Fine. I'm going.

The march was short, as Kelly's house was one of the few outside the village limits nearer the shoreline, and yet in her perception it seemed to last forever. With each step, her legs felt heavier.

But soon enough, the outlines of the misty Black Isles came into view in the distance, illuminated only by moonlight. The crisp, cold sea shimmered in the light, like diamonds. Not that Kelly had ever seen a real diamond before, but she'd heard it said they were even shinier than fresh ice.

A glimmer of curiosity overcame her. That was where she was headed; if she was to believe the stories. What secrets did those dark rocks out in the Northern Sea hide? Nothing good, for sure.

The villagers surrounding her had initially seemed calm and reserved, but now on the rocky beach, their faces had become tenser, more nervous. *Typical*, Kelly thought, *I'm the one being served up to the barbaric giants, and they're the ones who are scared.*

The butcher's large, calloused hands seemed to be trembling slightly as he attached the rope from Kelly's wrist to the huge iron ring on the half-eroded sacrificial post. He didn't even meet Kelly's gaze, which despite the incoming darkness was burning with anger and betrayal. Her earlier tears had long faded in the harsh wind. All that remained was a growing urge to fight.

She'd find a way to escape. She had to.

"Sorry, lass. May God be with ya," he whispered, before joining the procession again, ready to retreat back to the village.

Kelly pressed her lips together. God had nothing to do with what was happening here. She watched scornfully as everyone backed away.

It was one of the rules of the ritual. No one shall remain with the offering. None shall lay eyes on the giants when they collect their prize.

Those rules were now etched into Kelly's mind, so often had she heard the stories. Every eight years, one of the coastal villages would put forth an offering. As prescribed, none of the girls had been seen since they were left at this exact spot.

This had been going on for as long as anyone in the village, even the elders, could remember.

All those lives ruined by such an archaic and stupid ritual!

There hadn't even been any sighting, any evidence that giants still roamed the Black Isles. None, except that the sacrificial post was always found empty the morning after an offering. Anyone could have taken those girls. Who knew what had become of them.

Kelly glared at the retreating villagers, last of whom was her father, who looked back once, but then hurried on home, or more likely, towards the tavern.

Bloody cowards, the lot of them.

How convenient to have a rule that nobody was allowed to stay and watch. Who knew who these giants actually were? Whether they even existed.

The last torch flickered away over the dune surrounding the beach, and the sound of the drum faded into the distance. The ritual was over, and life could go on as normal until eight years from now when another girl was to be chosen from a neighboring village.

But for Kelly, the night was far from over.

A dense fog had rolled in from the Northern Sea, covering the beach like a damp blanket. Kelly blinked a few times, but was unable to see a thing. How long had she been here for? Minutes, hours? It was impossible to tell, although dawn still seemed impossibly far away.

Mother, don't leave me here.

Kelly's eyelids grew too heavy to remain open.

My darling, rest. You'll need it, a familiar voice seemed to say.

Mother! Was she dreaming already?

The regular crashing of waves had already hypnotized her. One could only be upset for so long, until it took a toll. Kelly tried her best to lift the heavy blanket of exhaustion; to stay alert. But it was hopeless. It would take a lot more than some fog to scare her awake.

CHAPTER TWO

———◆———

Broc held on to his sword tightly, the leather of his gloves creaking loudly under his powerful grip. He could hear it, despite the screeching winds and waves battering the wooden boat.

Although they were at peace with the men of West Hythe, one could never be too careful.

Every eight years, the humans had held up their end of the bargain, though. They had left a suitable young woman behind on the shore near their villages, and nobody had stayed behind to watch the giants' arrival or possibly interfere.

In any case, the timing of this exchange was carefully thought out: nights on the Northern Sea were always foggy this time of year. If anyone had stayed behind, they would have to be very nearby indeed to be able to see a thing. Looking around the wooden longship, Broc could see a lot of his people were much more excited about tonight's festivities than he was. Their chatter was even louder than the rhythmic drum setting the speed for the rowers. He hated to have to do this; to tear a young girl away from the only life she had known and take her to the Isles against her will. Sadly there was no other way to ensure the survival of their bloodline; without this tradition, Broc's people might become even extinct.

After the Great War, many of their number had fallen. Outnumbered, and overpowered by the sorcerers who had sided with humankind, their kind had retreated to the Black Isles and left the mainland to be ruled by men. However, their reduced numbers had meant that they would need fresh blood to replenish their line.

One can only interbreed for so long before things start to go wrong and madness sets in.

He had seen it happen with his own two eyes. If he squinted, he could just about see the shore through the dense fog. Luckily, his people had a lot better vision than the humans, meaning they could safely navigate the treacherous waters around Hythe Bay to collect the latest addition to their clan.

Broc had first pick, as was tradition.

There was no way he could get out of it either. He'd been king of the Black Mountain and surrounding isles for seven years, ever since his father had sailed off into the next realm.

It was time to start thinking about an heir, whether he liked it or not.

"Wonder what this one's going to be like," Rhea next to him remarked, her tone sharp with spite. Her comment was a reference to the trouble they'd had last time. Transitions could be difficult.

He glanced over at the strong young princess, his cousin twice removed, as she stared darkly over the water leading to the coast. It was obvious she'd wanted to be his queen, but it wasn't meant to be. A union between them would have been forbidden, in any case.

They were too closely related. And they even shared the same animal form.

Broc had always aimed to be a fair ruler; he could not make an exception to such an important rule for himself. The consequences would be too severe; the islanders' mating rules existed for a reason.

A king must do everything within his power to ensure a healthy heir is produced. In his case this had meant taking a human as his bride instead of the relative he'd grown up with. Although he hadn't made his intentions about this Reaping public yet, Rhea had guessed. And she had made it a point to openly express her displeasure.

Shortly before the keel of their ship threatened to hit ground, Teaq, Broc's half-brother and commander of the Black Isle armies, gave the order to steady the oars and drop anchor. Impeccable timing as always.

Broc observed as Rhea and Teaq shared a dark look. It was obvious they each disapproved of tonight's goings on for their own reasons.

"There she is," Teaq spat, unable to disguise his disgust.

His tone rubbed Broc the wrong way. It wasn't the girl's fault she had been sent to them as an offering in the Reaping. And what exactly had sparked Teaq's dislike of human females, Broc had not yet understood. "Remember, she will be shown the respect deserving of any citizen of the Black Isles," Broc spoke in a low, determined tone.

Teaq's jaw tensed, but he did not respond. "Yes, my king." Rhea averted her eyes from the shore and retreated to the back of the ship to stand watch over the waters behind them. As commander of the royal guard, it was her duty to ensure Broc wasn't ambushed.

"Just remember what we discussed," Teaq grumbled. "These are troubled times. The last thing we need is further complications within our own walls."

Broc nodded.

When their father had conducted the last Reaping ritual, the girl had found it incredibly difficult to adjust to her new surroundings. For some time it was feared they'd lose her to madness, but thankfully she had recovered and integrated into their way of life some months later.

They'd instituted a new rule; the newcomer would not be fully introduced into their ways until she had obviously adjusted to her new circumstances. Teaq had wanted for things to go much further; including keeping the girl on house arrest for the first month; something Broc had vehemently disagreed with. As king, the final decision had obviously been his.

They would keep her in the dark, figuratively, but she would be as free as any of the other inhabitants of the Black Isles. At least as far as her movements within the castle on Black Mountain were concerned.

Still, it was for the best to be cautious. She did not need

to know the truth about everything from the start. Humans did not handle it well when their views of the world were challenged.

"I wish you'd reconsider and at least let me put a watch on her. We do not know of her intentions," Teaq added.

Broc scoffed. *Her intentions.* This was just going to be some unfortunate girl who thought she was being sent to her death.

Just like the last ones.

Lately Teaq had grown more and more paranoid. They had enough to worry about with the threats from further out at sea. As long as the humans continued to hold up their end of the truce, their peace would hold.

"Alright. That's enough of that," Broc said. "We've laid down the rules already. But I won't have her treated as a prisoner under my rule. Let's get on with what we came here to do."

The many dozen or so soldiers onboard held their heads bowed as Broc strode past towards the port beam, which was by now perfectly lined up with the shoreline. Teaq signaled the all clear and jumped over the side, landing squarely on his feet in the waist-deep water. Broc followed.

They were back on track, but this wasn't the end of that particular discussion; Broc was certain of it. Teaq's stubbornness was in part because as the older brother he'd always expected to get first right to the throne. He wasn't good at following orders.

Too bad for him that their father, the late King Ryk, hadn't seen it that way. They had fought it out just like in the old days. Hand-to-hand combat.

Obviously, it was Broc's victory that had earned him the honor of ruling over the Black Isles. Whether Teaq liked it or not.

The salty water of the Northern Sea was close to freezing, but Broc—as well as the rest of his clan—were used to it. They were much better suited to cold temperatures than humans were.

Despite the saltiness in the air, Broc could smell the human from across the stony beach. Her scent was sweet, almost floral, with a hint of something sharp. Fear, perhaps.

His inner beast stirred. A new sort of sensation came over him. Although he hadn't even seen her yet, he knew how this Reaping was going to end. She would be his. And she would give him his much awaited heir. It was a bittersweet prospect.

The poor girl had no idea what was in store for her. Teaq took the lead, and Broc, flanked by two of his guards, followed towards the wooden post in the distance. Rhea stayed behind the men, keeping watch over the waters that separated them and the ship. The guards as well as Teaq had drawn their swords, just in case. Though the girl's was the only human scent in the air, they were trained never to make assumptions when it came to the king's safety.

Eight years since they'd last come here. King Ryk had been in charge of the last Reaping. How much had changed. Broc could now see the outline of a figure through the fog. She was tall for a human, though still a good two feet shorter than him, and clad in an ankle length cloak of some sort. Her curly hair blew wildly in the harsh wind, but there was no movement in her otherwise. Still, he could hear her heartbeat over the loud breeze. It was strong and regular; indicating that she was in good physical health.

As they covered the last few feet between them, her sweet scent almost overwhelmed his senses.

"Hold on." Teaq gestured at Broc to wait behind him, but Broc was similarly bad at following orders. "What's your name, girl?" Teaq demanded, as he towered over her.

The general's harsh tone startled the girl, causing her to let out a quick yelp. Although she was now shivering in the cold wind, she didn't cower like Broc had come to expect from previous offerings. After the initial shock of finding herself no longer alone on the windswept beach, she had recovered quickly.

Broc suppressed a smile. Teaq's attempt to intimidate her had failed.

"Kelly," she said in a firm voice. "Kelly Chaslain."

This was ridiculous. There was no threat here. "Well then, Kelly Chaslain of West Hythe." Broc stepped forward, and signaled Teaq to remove her bonds, who grudgingly obliged.

"I am Broc Bearclaw, King of the Black Isles." She blinked at him a few times, her eyes glazed over and dull; her eyelids were heavy with exhaustion. Poor girl, she must have had quite the ordeal behind her already. Still, she was in excellent shape, all things considered. "And now you are coming with us," Broc said. "So it's true," she whispered, before her eyes closed and her knees gave way underneath her.

Broc reacted quickly and caught her, just about. He wrapped her up in her woolen cloak and lifted her up in his arms.

How tiny and fragile she was.

Just at that moment, the fog lifted just enough to let some moonlight filter through. Her complexion shone almost white, her face flawless and unscarred, surrounded by a fiery red mane the likes of which Broc had never seen before.

Of all the human women he had ever laid eyes on, not one had been as enthralling.

The vision before him almost made him forget his reservations about the Reaping ritual. *Almost.*

He caught himself a couple of seconds later, and forced his gaze away from Kelly's unconscious form.

Broc nodded at Teaq and the guards.

It's time to leave. They turned, retreating towards the ship with their latest clan member: Broc's new queen, Kelly

16

Chaslain of West Hythe. Undoubtedly the most beautiful human alive.

Would she adapt to their ways? Would she accept her role by his side as queen of the Black Isles? Would his people accept *her* as such?

Only time would tell.

CHAPTER THREE

———◆———

$\mathcal{S}$hadows circled Kelly. Inhumanly large figures, entirely in black. The clanging of weaponry and armor. A flag, flapping overhead, attempting to compete with the crashing waves.

But among all the confusion, there was something familiar. A smiling face. Red hair like her own.

You're not alone. You're safe here.

"Mother?"

Kelly startled awake, and covered her mouth with both hands to stop herself from screaming. Her heart beat so hard, the sound of it seemed to echo against the walls of the cell she found herself in.

She closed her eyes again and inhaled deeply. The memory of her dreams was already fading. Where was she?

Kelly blinked a few times. Her surroundings were unfamiliar. The dark, almost black stone walls looked like they belonged to a castle, not an ordinary building like the ones in her village. The bed she'd found herself in was much bigger than normal, both in width as well as length, meaning she had at least three feet of space below her feet despite being fully stretched out.

Even the heavy wooden door was impossibly tall. There was not much light, no windows that she could see, just a flaming torch attached to an iron fitting on the wall.

CLAIMED BY THE KING

They had taken her. The giants that came to the beach.

She was on the Black Isles somewhere. A barren rock in the middle of the Northern Sea.

Kelly rubbed her eyes, and tried to remember what exactly had happened. The last thing she recalled was a face appearing above her in the dark of the misty beach. Two black eyes, set deeply in an angular, masculine face. His full beard covered part of a scar that extended from his high and pronounced cheekbone down to God only knows where.

It was the face of her captor: Broc Bearclaw. King of the Black Isles.

Everything after that was so fuzzy, it was beyond her reach.

Remembering his introduction gave her shivers all the way down her spine. She had tried not to show fear, to appear brave, but his deep, almost threatening voice had made her weak inside. And that was ignoring how impossibly tall he was.

Of course they're tall. They're giants, after all!

Now that she was alone, recounting these events in her head, she was second-guessing everything that had happened during their first encounter. Why on earth had she introduced herself with her mother's maiden name rather than her own family name? What difference did a name make when you were going to be a prisoner, anyway?

All she could recall was that saying her mother's name aloud had given her some semblance of strength. If only she had still been alive today, she would have never allowed Kelly to be taken as a sacrifice. All Kelly had for support was that name.

Kelly shook her head. She had to focus, if she was going to get through this somehow.

She looked around again.

This room where she had been left almost seemed too comfortable considering her desperate situation. She was their prisoner now, their slave, and yet, the bed on which they laid her down was more comfortable than the small cot she'd shared with Ferris for as long as she could remember.

She leaned up on both elbows and noticed that she was no longer wearing the same clothing as last night. Instead of her sensible long frock, with the woolen cloak, she was now clad in a soft, shimmery nightgown. The thought of someone taking her clothes off while she was unconscious made her feel even more vulnerable. She could only hope these people—no, these giants, had made a female perform that particular task, otherwise the shame would be unbearable.

They *had* females here, didn't they?

Her thoughts were interrupted by a loud metallic click and the creaking of the door. Quickly, Kelly dropped back into her soft pillow and closed her eyes, pretending to still be sleeping.

"Aw, look at that, she's still resting," a deep, yet unmistakably female voice said.

Kelly breathed a near silent sigh of relief. At least it wasn't the king, or the other, even scarier giant who had collected her from the shore.

"Humans… And to think that *they* won the mainland, whereas we have to live on this miserable rock in the water," another female sneered.

Kelly's heartbeat sped up so much, it was almost deafening in her own ears. Still, she didn't move a muscle.

After she heard the clanging of metallic objects near her, two sets of footsteps shuffled away and the door creaked again, shutting with the same metallic click.

Carefully, she opened her eyes and noticed a platter with a dome shaped cover on the table beside her. She lifted it and immediately the delicious scent of bacon entered her nostrils. Her stomach spasmed painfully, reminding her of how hungry she was. Although she had planned to be cautious, she couldn't resist.

She'd need her energy if she wanted to escape later. At least that was her justification. Surely they wouldn't have brought her here just to poison her first meal?

So she ate like it was her last meal on earth, because perhaps, it would be. Once they noticed she was awake, who knew what would happen.

Surprisingly, the food was amazing. Kelly hadn't considered that a bunch of barbarians living out in the sea would know good food when they saw it.

Yet the bacon, as well as the bread, were as good, if not better than what she had grown up with. On those rare occasions her family could afford bacon, that was. Their staple fare had been eggs from their own chickens, and stew made of the various vegetables that grew on their land.

A pig was a rare and prized possession on the mainland. Not many could afford it.

As soon as she had finished dabbing up the last crumbs of food from the pewter plate with her finger tip, something stirred in the dark far corner of the room. She was so startled she dropped the platter, which made an almighty racket upon hitting the stone floor.

That part of the room was so dark, she hadn't noticed anything—or anyone—there before.

"Well," that same impossibly deep voice she'd heard when they picked her up at the beach said. "At least you've got a good appetite. Not like the last one."

With a loud creak, the figure stood up from what must have been a big chair or bench hidden in the shadows.

Kelly was breathless and terrified, as she tried to scurry away backwards. The headboard prevented any further retreat.

The large outline of the giant man came into view, details on his strange attire shimmering in the dim light of the torch on the wall as he approached.

Broc, the king of the giants, Kelly remembered.

"How long have you been watching?" Kelly stammered.

"I entered with Rhea and Bree when they brought in the food."

Kelly blinked at him in disbelief. He snuck in with the two females? She hadn't heard his footsteps, or noticed his presence at all.

"We can be stealthy when we want to be," the man grinned, making something inside Kelly's chest stir.

Although he was terrifyingly tall, and built like an ox, now in the privacy of this room, his face wasn't as menacing and scary as it had seemed in the darkness of the beach. The warm light from the torch on the wall helped.

"I see."

"Now that you're awake, perhaps you ought to get dressed and get to know your new family." The way he spoke suggested a certain unexpected warmth. After all the stories she'd heard growing up of the barbaric giants, she hadn't considered that they were capable of compassion.

"What's going to happen to me?" Kelly whispered, still confused about what fate would be in store for her.

"I understand this isn't what you wanted for yourself. Believe me if there was another way, we'd do away with the Reaping ritual." Broc paused for a moment, then added, "Where we take in a human girl once every eight years."

Kelly slowly shook her head, no, this wasn't how she'd

wanted her life to turn out.

"It's a necessity for us, for our survival. But you'll learn about that soon enough. What matters is that you're safe here. You'll not be harmed."

Another sigh of relief escaped her lips before she could regain her composure.

Kelly suddenly remembered the voice she'd heard in her dreams. Her mother's voice.

You're safe here.

He sounded genuine, and she desperately wanted to believe him. She had worried so much already. She was exhausted.

If he was speaking the truth, perhaps she should go along with it all to gain the giants' trust and an opportunity to escape would present itself soon enough. Whether they were compassionate or not, she still had no intention of staying on this island any longer than necessary.

Broc turned and reached the door in barely two strides, turning back just once. "Bree left a few things for you in the wardrobe. I can send her in to help dress you."

Remembering the sharp comments from the two women who had brought her food, she quickly shook her head.

"No, I think I'd prefer to get ready on my own."

Broc shrugged, then turned the iron handle on the door, opening it with the same almighty creak it had made before.

He'd lock it from the outside, no doubt. There'd be no point in trying to open it myself once he's gone, Kelly thought glumly.

As soon as the large wooden structure clicked back into place, Kelly attempted to stretch the lingering exhaustion out of her tired shoulders. Passing out from fear did not make for a good rest.

She turned, and hung her legs down the side of the bed, noting that it was quite a bit taller than beds were back home. *Of course it was.*

Everything was bigger here, including the people.

Kelly took a few careful steps towards the large wardrobe, also in the dark corner of the room, and waited for her eyesight to adjust. The cold of the stone floor stung the bottom of her feet, but at least the air wasn't too chilly, letting her take her time rifling through the unfamiliar fabrics hidden behind the wardrobe's beautifully carved doors. Eventually, she picked out a gown of sorts that wasn't as elaborate as most of the others, though without taking it over to the bed, she couldn't make out exactly what color it was. How did these people live in these dark and gloomy conditions? Did they not need to see?

She stumbled back into the light and lay the gown across her mattress to take a better look.

It was a deep burgundy, like poppies about to wilt. She ran her fingertips over the smooth fabric down the front, as well as the intricate metallic looking embroidery at the neck line. She'd never seen a dress this ornate and elegant before. It was certainly vastly different from the plain woolens she was accustomed to wearing.

Turning it over, she noticed there was a lace-up back, and suddenly Kelly regretted refusing the help she'd been offered. Disappointed, she went back to the wardrobe, picking out another two gowns, a black one and a golden one. Upon closer inspection the latter seemed a bit more loose fitting and easier to manage on her own.

Kelly put it on, and bemoaned the lack of a mirror in the room. She could only hope she looked somewhat presentable. The moment she had finished adjusting the braided belt around her waist, the door clicked again and revealed the tallest woman Kelly had ever seen.

"My name is Bree, I'm supposed to assist you in any way possible. Your name is Kelly Chaslain, am I right?"

The woman, Bree, towered almost a foot over Kelly, who was already above average height compared to the other girls from her village.

Kelly nodded, but was lost for words otherwise.

"Broc requests your presence in the main hall. I see you're already dressed. Good. Will you follow me?"

Looking back at the two discarded gowns on the bed, Kelly hesitated.

"Don't worry, I'll take care of those, Kelly Chaslain," Bree said with a smile.

"Thanks," Kelly mumbled, "You can just call me Kelly." She clumsily followed Bree toward the door. It took her almost four steps to cross the same distance the king had previously travelled in just two steps.

It occurred to Kelly that she had felt out of place most her life, because she was broader, taller and not as delicate as the other girls. Yet here, on the Black Isles, she felt so small. Under any other circumstances, the entire situation would almost be funny.

CHAPTER FOUR

roc's position at the head of the main banquet table was perfect to oversee the rowdy company he found himself in. His subjects were in a very good mood indeed.

He himself had been thoughtful, until movement at the other end of the hall caught his attention.

Suddenly it became easy to ignore the goings-on around him, as Kelly, his human, walked into the Great Hall. A vision in gold, the new dress she had worn had transformed her from the diamond in the rough they'd found on the beach to a jewel worthy of kings. Even her mannerisms had changed, or so it seemed, as she elegantly placed one foot in front of the other, reluctantly heading towards Broc's throne.

She was tall, for a human, and her figure was unlike any of the Black Isle females. Soft curves, rather than hard muscle, hidden underneath the delicate, flowing fabric of her gown... Watching her made him forget his aversion to this particular tradition.

She was to be his bride, no question about it, and at this time he did not feel unease, but pride instead. Through their interaction earlier, he had also seen that she wasn't as meek and fearful as he had expected human females to be. Of course his presence had startled her, but her questions suggested curiosity rather than despair. With a bit of luck she would adjust quickly; learn their ways and make them her own.

Then, they could learn all there was to know about one another. Even Black Isle's biggest secret.

Broc continued to watch as Bree guided the human through the crowd of men and women, who were already well underway in their celebrations. The Reaping had always been an occasion for everyone; an excuse for a lavish celebration that would last for days, commemorating the new addition to their clan and the promise of their continued survival.

It was a welcome change from their daily routine. It wasn't easy, feeding the giant appetites of the islanders. And on top of that they had to continue defending their territory, as well as the mainland, from the threats that originated further out to sea.

His people had a lot going for them, but an easy peace was not one of them.

"Please, join us." Broc waved Kelly over towards the seat to his left. The ornately carved chair wasn't as imposing as his own throne, but it was appropriate for her future position in his court.

The much cruder seat to the right of course was already occupied by Teaq, who despite the promise of ale to mark this joyous occasion could not stop himself from glaring at the human. Thankfully she seemed not to take notice.

Kelly nodded and clambered backwards onto her chair, her face reddening when she finally met Broc's stare.

"It's a little tall," she explained dryly, before smoothing down her dress and diverting her gaze toward the festivities going on in the rest of the hall.

Broc could not suppress a smile. The human, she seemed to have a sense of humor.

"Although the feast is about to begin, I felt it prudent to send you some breakfast. You had been sleeping for quite a while," he said, changing the topic.

Kelly looked up at him in surprise. "How long?"

"A day." Noting the shock in Kelly's eyes, he added, "Don't worry, it's not uncommon during the transition." She opened her mouth slightly, as though she wanted to say something, but their moment of quiet was interrupted by an outburst from the crowd seated in front of them.

"What are we waiting for?" someone shouted.

"We want more ale!"

The islanders roared and some banged their empty tankards rhythmically onto the battered wooden tables in front of them.

"And wine!" one of the older members of the castle guard shouted, while raising a pewter chalice up into the air.

Even the small group of normally very sedate Elders was starting to become vocal.

Broc got up from his throne, his hands raised in an attempt to control the commotion.

"My dear men and women of Black Isle. Settle down!" Broc spoke with authority, without raising his voice much. Still, quiet spread around the hall as his subjects found their way back to their seats.

"Tonight we celebrate a new Reaping!" Again, the crowd cheered, some of the more excitable men clanging the butts of their swords or axes against the tables and benches.

"As you know, it has been eight years since our people have been blessed with new blood. The last time the lucky man was Elog of the Shard." Broc raised his tankard, his gesture mirrored by his followers. "And we all know how that turned out!"

Broc's latter remark sparked cheers, whistles and laughter.

"Bastard hardly leaves the house, I hear," Teaq remarked. Despite his still grim expression, he got up and clanged his tankard to Broc's.

"To Elog!" Teaq cheered, before sitting back down.

"Five beautiful children!" Broc exclaimed, met by an even bigger ruckus from the crowd. "To ensure the future of our clan!"

"May all our unions be as fruitful!" a booming voice shouted from across the room.

"May our ranks swell to their former glory!" the crowd responded in unison.

"May our honor be restored!" Broc replied. "Let the

feast begin!"

As soon as Broc finished speaking and sat back down in his ceremonial seat, some of the seated giants got up and vanished through the double doors towards the side of the hall, before re-emerging with trays laden with roast wild boar, smoked whole fish, lobsters and other seafood, as well as breads of varying shapes and colors. Numerous barrels of ale and wine were rolled in, one of each per table, and empty tankards and platters travelled the lengths of the crowd back and forth until everyone's plates were full and the feast could begin.

"Here you go," Bree said as she approached Kelly, handing her a large chalice.

The latter seemed taken aback by the festivities unfolding in front of her. She was observing everything and everyone with wide, curious eyes.

"Don't worry." Broc leaned over and tried to reassure her. "They're a good bunch. Our circumstances don't permit celebrations like this too often so we try to make the most of it."

"What circumstances are those?" Kelly asked. Broc's expression turned serious. The firmness in her voice had surprised him.

"We may be in the midst of a truce with the people of West Hythe, but life on a rock in the middle of the Northern Sea is far from easy or peaceful." He averted his gaze from hers, staring darkly in the distance. "There are things out there which the humans on the mainland couldn't dream up in their worst nightmares."

Teaq, who seemingly had just begun listening in on their conversation, subtly shook his head, probably as a warning.

Broc responded with a very brief and very silent glare. He watched as Teaq got up and left the table to join Rhea, who had taken a seat at the other end of the hall.

Just as well. If the two of them wanted to brood throughout the Reaping feast, that was their own choice. They might make a fine couple one day, if only they could get over their stubbornness.

"We tend to be preoccupied with what's on the Black Isles themselves," Kelly remarked.

This single statement drew Broc back into their conversation. What did the humans know of the Black Isles beyond what had been written into the treaty so many generations ago? The previous offerings had precious little knowledge of where they were being sent.

"How so?" he asked.

"Only last year, a young boy vanished while out crabbing at the bay. All that remained of him was the jute sack containing his catch for the day. Blood stained." "And your people believe *we* were responsible?" Broc squinted at Kelly, curious how she might respond. Things were getting interesting now.

"Well you like your meat, don't you? That's what's been

said. That after growing tired of the taste of fish, the giants of Black Isle have developed a taste for human flesh." Kelly spoke in such a matter-of-fact fashion it sounded almost flippant.

Broc was surprised at her candor. Who would willingly divulge such a terrible story to the very same people who were supposedly responsible? Or did she have her own doubts about the truth in her tale and was just testing the waters?

"Human flesh isn't all it's cracked up to be. We much prefer wild boar when the craving for meat strikes us." Broc kept his expression straight as he raised up his plate as a form of proof.

Kelly, who had just taken a sip of her wine, seemed completely unfazed by the turn of their conversation. "I'm glad to hear it."

When their eyes met, he thought he could detect a hint of   amusement. This human sure was different. A morbid sense of humor was something usually reserved for those hardened in battle. And Kelly, much like the other women who had joined their clan over the years, did not look like much of a fighter.

"After the feast, I would like to show you around if that's agreeable to you," Broc said.

Kelly nodded, and broke off a piece of bread from the platter that was currently making the rounds on their table. "I would like that very much, thank you."

They did not speak much for the remainder of the meal; the loud celebrations surrounding them prevented it. When Teaq returned with a fresh cask of ale, Broc figured it was just as well.

Still, he caught himself glancing over at his future companion, wondering what was going on in her head. He hadn't mentioned his intentions to her, yet, instead reserving that topic for a more appropriate time. Would she be agreeable?

His inner beast insisted she would have to be.

A blush had crept over her cheeks and the sweet, floral scent he had first noticed on the beach continued to tempt him even now. The celebration had suited her.

Broc tried to shake these observations for the time being and instead enjoy the evening, as Kelly seemed to do.

By the time the food had all but been finished, and the casks of ale and wine were near empty, the Reaping feast had progressed to the next stage, song.

Ancient melodies flooded the hall and those with good singing voices added the lyrics. The songs told of legendary battles, of the invasion of the mainland by the humans. Of sorcery and monsters living deep underneath the sea.

Some even told of his own people and their secrets; though the words were poetic and deliberately vague. *Taming one's inner beast*; that could be interpreted in any number of ways.

He noticed Kelly softly tapping her fingers along with the rhythm of the music.

Did they tell these same stories in West Hythe?

Did the humans, Kelly included, realize they weren't *just* stories?

If Kelly had any suspicions about the true nature of the people of the Black Isles, she certainly knew how to hide it.

Some of the men and women got up to dance, but Broc himself was content as an observer. Maybe he'd have the opportunity to dance with *her* one of these days. Once the uncertainty was over, and there were no more secrets between him and his future bride.

This was not that day.

CHAPTER FIVE

hat was she thinking? Kelly couldn't believe she had just told the story of little Timothy's disappearance, all but accusing Broc and his clan of eating the boy alive.

It must have been the wine. Surely that, or whatever strange exhaustion that had overwhelmed her on the beach. Apparently it was all normal during her transition, whatever that meant.

Thankfully it seemed Broc had taken it well enough. His remark about wild boar had almost sounded like a joke, though she couldn't be certain.

For the remainder of the feast, she tried to keep her head down, and her conversation to a minimum to avoid further awkwardness. Thankfully the crowd started to sing soon after, eliminating the chance for further chats.

She was surprised to find that these barbarians were seemingly less cannibalistic than the stories of the village elders had made them appear. They also had great taste in food and wine.

Especially the latter had a very agreeable flavor, not too much of a burn, certainly not as sharp as the stuff her father used to drink when he thought she had gone to bed already. After only a few sips, she stopped feeling the slight chill coming off the dark granite walls of the Great Hall, her body instead filled with a pleasing warmth and cheeriness that seemed completely inappropriate for someone in her situation.

From what she had gathered during Broc's speech earlier, it seemed her role was not at all like that of a normal slave or prisoner. She was going to be a kept woman, responsible for providing healthy heirs for one of these wildlings. The fact that Broc had taken a personal interest in her and even made her sit by his side suggested she was going to be his bride.

This thought ought to fill her with dread, but somehow, their interactions had had a calming effect on her.

He had been respectful and decent, not aggressive and intimidating like some of the others. *Imagine if it had been the other giant, Teaq…* Kelly shuddered at the thought.

She couldn't help but steal a glance at the huge man by her side. She had never met any nobleman, never mind a king, but she imagined in the human world a feast like this would be conducted very differently.

The giants seemed to treat each other mostly as equals. Everyone, even the men, served each other when another's plate became empty. They treated each other as a family, with Broc firmly at the helm yet not exempt from jokes or even criticism.

It was a strange sight to behold, especially when it was a male offering a refilled glass or plate to a female. This type of thing would never happen in her village. There, especially the tavern was off limits for females, except for the beer wenches that worked there, whose position was certainly not enviable or respected.

Women were expected to take care of the home, while men went out and reaped the benefits of their farming or fishing efforts. That was the way things had always been as far as Kelly knew.

On this dark, cold island in the middle of the sea, everything she thought she knew about the world seemed obsolete. Her thoughts were interrupted by the occasional loud remark or question directed at Broc, which he responded to in the same controlled, quiet manner he adopted in all of his interactions.

He seemed like a good leader, well respected by almost everyone except perhaps Teaq, who Kelly had learned was his brother.

After a few rounds of drinks, even Teaq had cast off his earlier bad mood and properly joined in the celebrations. The dirty looks in Kelly's direction had also subsided as the night grew darker.

Perhaps she had been too quick to judge the giants, based on the snide remark she'd overheard in her room earlier. And of course, the better part of two decades listening to stories the villagers of West Hythe had told over open fires.

All this could still be just a ruse to get her to feel comfortable. However, Kelly doubted anyone, especially these exuberant people, could act so well while imbibing this much liquor.

Just the one glass full had gone to her own head significantly.

After listening to the various conversations and introductions over the past two hours, she now knew a few of the faces surrounding her a little better. There was Teaq of course, the commander in charge of Broc's army, Rhea, Broc's cousin and the most fearsome female Kelly had ever seen. Rhea also seemed the most disapproving of Kelly's presence, though Kelly still had no idea what caused her offense.

Broc had introduced her to some of the others at the first table as well, but she couldn't recall their names anymore. They all looked and acted alike, the only notable differences between them their different lengths and shades of facial hair.

At one end of the hall sat a few white-haired men in pale grey robes. The giants' elders. Kelly couldn't help but wonder how old they were. Their skin was so wrinkled and fragile. Like flakes of ash, about to turn to dust. And their beards, white as snow.

None of the senior inhabitants of West Hythe looked nearly as old as these men.

"If you're ready," Broc asked beside her.

She looked over at his outstretched hand and paused.

"I can show you around your new home now. They won't miss us." Unlike everyone around them, Broc was still his calm, controlled self. Either he'd not fully given in to the celebrations like the others, or he must have had an incredible amount of self-discipline not to let it show.

Kelly nodded and slid off her chair, accepting Broc's hand to keep her steady.

That wine really had been quite strong. She took a deep breath and focused on placing one foot ahead of the other, while keeping her head high as to not show weakness. Thankfully the floor did not feel quite as cold as it had before.

In fact she could not really feel her feet at all anymore. It was like she was floating.

Broc adjusted his long strides to match her pace better as they weaved past the banquet tables where the other giants were still eating, drinking and making merry.

A guard opened the large double doors at the side of the main hall and Broc and Kelly stepped into a dark corridor lined with the occasional torch on the wall. These giants really needed to address their lighting situation. The dim glow of the torches was not enough for her poor eyes.

Kelly was apprehensive about where they were headed, but then reconciled herself with the fact that if Broc had any ill will towards her, there was nothing she could do about it. She was at his mercy, so she might as well not worry about it.

After making it to the end of the corridor, around a couple of corners, Broc led her through a doorway, where all of a sudden a gust of wind chilled her to her core.

The vista stretched out ahead of her was breathtaking. Dramatic grey clouds lined with silver where the moonlight passed by them; the gurgling dark waters below seemed to hide all manner of evil. They stood quite high up on a plateau of stone surrounded by a fortified wall just low enough for her to peer over, yet high enough to keep her from being swept up by the wind.

Despite the cold, and the powerful gusts, Kelly stepped forward and placed her hands on the cold stone wall, allowing her to lean forward slightly. Perhaps a hundred feet below the platform, Kelly could make out the rocky mass of the island which the fortress had been built upon. The seas ahead of them were broken apart by the occasional sharp cluster of rocks, shiny yet black in the subdued moonlight.

"It seemed prudent to take you here first. On a calm day the mainland is visible from here, but not on a night like tonight." Broc looked down at her.

Perhaps still due to the wine, she broke character and met his gaze directly. His eyes were still black, but there was nothing dark or ominous about them this time. She thought she could see a certain kindness in them, along with a fiery warmth that set her heart alight.

How was it possible that this giant, this warrior who should instill fear in her, seemed so welcoming and even friendly? How could she possibly continue to distrust someone with such honest eyes? And yet how could she possibly put her faith in someone who would abduct a girl such as herself once every eight years just because it was written into a treaty?

None of it made any sense.

Broc broke eye contact at last, and cleared his throat.

"You must be freezing. Let us continue on." Broc placed his large hand on the back of Kelly's shoulder, sending an even more intense shiver down her spine than the icy winds had already done. Although she found it hard to let go of the impressive view, she did allow herself to be guided back indoors.

The rest of their stroll around the imposing castle was mostly quiet, except for the occasional explanation from Broc. All of it, from the stairs leading down to the dungeons, the wing set into the mountain containing the chambers of everyone who lived here, right up to the drawbridge and gate that led to the harbor, merged into one in Kelly's mind. There was no chance of her ever finding her way around this place. There were no markings to remember anything by. All corridors, rooms constructed out of granite blocks, or sometimes hewn straight into the mountain itself, looked too alike.

And all of it was barely lit up.

Kelly felt her eyes grow heavier and heavier as they walked through the maze of stone. Her supposed new home, until she could find a way off the island, that was.

At last they stopped in front of yet another ten foot tall

wooden door with iron hinges that looked identical to all the other ten foot tall wooden doors with iron hinges Kelly had seen this evening.

"Your chambers," Broc said, as he turned the handle with the click and creak she had become familiar with earlier in the evening. "I'd lead you back to the feast, but you look exhausted."

Kelly stood confused for a moment, staring at the door first, then looking inside the room to convince herself that it was actually where she had woken up. No guards at the door? Not even a bolt on the outside? How was it possible that they'd kept her, a prisoner, here against her will, in a completely unsecured room on her own? What if she had tried to run immediately after getting up?

"Thank you," Kelly stammered, but suddenly her legs refused to move and she froze as if her feet had grown roots.

"Where are your chambers?" she finally asked.

Broc responded with a knowing smile and nodded his head towards a door just down the hallway towards the right of her room. The last door on this end of the corridor. "Only a few steps away."

Kelly bowed her head as she entered her bedroom, thanking Broc again for his hospitality, upon which he left, closing the door behind him.

The evening's events had sent her thoughts into a confused frenzy. She was going to be his woman, whether she wanted to or not. So why not just get right to it and claim her? Why all the politeness? If they hadn't shared that intense stare out on the lookout point earlier, she may have suspected that he had no interest in her. Clearly, he had.

Oh Mother, what is the purpose of it all?

Kelly closed her eyes and tried to make sense of everything that had happened to her so far. But this was not something she could unravel here on her own.

CHAPTER SIX

———— • ————

Broc knew his approach with Kelly was out of the ordinary. If for example Teaq been awarded a human bride, he would have just been his obnoxious self until she agreed to see things his way. He may have even forced himself on the girl if that was what it took.

His brother had never been the subtle kind. However, Broc could not bring himself to do it. He preferred to let nature run its course first to see where it would lead him with Kelly. There was no rush, yet. And if he had interpreted their moment on the Watch Point correctly, he was already gaining ground with her. When he surprised her earlier in the evening in her chambers, she had been afraid of him, obviously. But by the time he showed her the view from on top of the castle fortifications, something about her had changed. The way she had looked at him betrayed something other than distrust and hostility.

Perhaps all of this was just a fantasy on his part. A dream inspired by that first moment when he saw his future bride at the beach. An infatuation, mudding his otherwise impeccable perception and ability to read people—allies and enemies alike.

But there definitely was something about her that he

could not yet understand. For a simple farmer's daughter from the mainland, she had shown incredible resilience, and bravery. Many a human entering into their world had spent the first weeks in despair, mourning the loss of life as she knew it. Kelly had shown none of that so far. Perhaps it was too early to tell.

Broc's thoughts were interrupted by the distant click of a door. He knew it to be Kelly's, and he knew that anyone other than him - namely Teaq - would have locked her up or at least posted a guard outside.

What would be the point? Where could she run to? If she even found her way to the harbor, she wouldn't do so undetected. And then, she wouldn't be able to sail to the mainland in these stormy conditions. The weather on the Northern Sea was treacherous in early spring and human females did not know how to sail alone. No, it would be fine. Let Kelly roam freely inside the castle for now, let her get used to her new surroundings until she could fully accept her place here.

He listened out for further noises, but couldn't hear a thing, not even footsteps. She must still be barefoot. He'd instruct Bree to provide her with some suitable footwear before they ventured outdoors.

Soon after Broc gave up on trying to hear further signs of her movements, he heard the creak of yet another door. His own.

He opened his eyes, his vision already accustomed to

the darkness of his room, and found Kelly's silhouette pausing in the entrance. She wouldn't be able to see a thing beyond the dimly glowing torch on the wall, giving him the advantage in this case.

"Broc, umm, your majesty," her soft voice called out. "I do apologize for disturbing you."

He sat up, surprised that she hadn't intended to keep her presence secret. Perhaps the clever girl had realized that there was no chance of surprising a battle hardened warrior such as Broc in his sleep.

"Just Broc is fine. What's the matter?"

"Would it be permissible for me to ask a few questions? After sleeping for a day already, it's impossible for me to find rest now."

Kelly stepped inside his room, while keeping her head lowered.

Broc got up to light a candle on the glowing torch on the wall, and noticed her gaze wandering from the corner of her eye. She spent a few moments stealthily looking around the large yet sparsely furnished room, then finally lingered on him.

"Shall I wait until you're dressed?" she asked, still unwilling to look at him directly for a long time, yet seemingly unable to contain her curiosity at his half-naked form.

He had always favored sleeping in only his breeches. The cold air of the unheated room did not bother him.

"You *assume* I was planning to get dressed." Broc kept a

straight face, even though his comment was meant in jest. If Kelly was shocked at his candor, she didn't show it. Instead she stepped forward a couple of paces, her relatively short human legs carrying her about half the distance a giant's stride would have.

Curiosity overcame him. *What was she doing here?*

"Your questions?" Broc asked, before taking a seat on the heavy chair beside his bed.

"What is my purpose… here?" Kelly folded her arms in front of her, then unfolded them again. Clearly, the girl was nervous but trying very hard not to let it show.

"Every eight years a human woman is offered up by the men of the mainland." Broc's explanation was intentionally vague; he was trying to test her reaction. "You know this." It took a few seconds of stark silence for her to formulate a follow-up question.

"Am I to be *your* woman?" she finally asked.

Broc couldn't suppress a smile. Indeed this one was quite different. Cautious when necessary, but of strong character and unusually direct. In a way she was a good match for his people. Islanders who didn't care much for false niceties and play acting.

It was a relief that she hadn't asked anything he would be unable to share during the transition.

"That depends."

Kelly shot him a curious look, before averting her eyes towards the floor again. "I do apologize if that was too forward. It was the only thing that made sense. Since I was seated beside you at the feast."

She paused.

"But your behavior puzzles me."

Broc got up from his seat and stepped towards the girl, who instinctively flinched backwards only slightly. An involuntary reflex.

"*My* behavior, you say." He reached for her, guiding Kelly's chin up towards him until she couldn't help but look up into his eyes. There was something there, when their eyes met, a spark, a glimmer of something he'd first felt when he'd collected her from that dark beach, not even two days ago.

This mysterious force seemed to grow with every moment he spent in her presence, making him question his patience, second-guessing his plan to woo her slowly. It was a powerful sensation which normally only songs were sung about, but which was rarely discussed in the open. The sacred bond between a man and woman who were meant to be.

As she blinked quicker than normal, her thick lashes momentarily hid her light green eyes from view. He heard her breathing pause, then speed up again.

She felt it too. He could tell.

"How would you have me behave, my lady?" Broc shot her the swiftest of smiles, so quick it would be easy to miss.

"That I do not know. But I know I didn't expect...

this." The way her shapely lips moved with every spoken word all but drove him crazy. His inner beast told him to pounce; an urge that became harder and harder to ignore as he continued to look into her eyes. But at the same time she spoke to his protective side. Those instincts that had served him well as King of the Black Isles, that had ensured the survival of his people through many a battle. Kelly's heartbeat grew more frantic with every passing moment, Broc could hear it so clearly. At the same time her eyes seemed to turn a darker shade of green as her pupils dilated. Broc had seen that same look on other people's faces. Couples, who could or would not hide their feelings for one another from the rest of the world. He could no longer fight his desires, and leaned down, bringing his face closer to hers until her eyes fluttered shut. She wanted him too, he could smell the change in her.

His normally controlled demeanor made way for something entirely new and reckless. It had been his self-control which had won him the throne, seven years ago. But faced with her, alone in his chambers during this quiet hour, he became a different man.

Broc gently touched his lips to hers, then gathered her up in his strong arms and carried her towards the bed. She embraced him and pressed herself tightly against his hard, muscular chest, all the while returning his kisses with a passion he had not foreseen.

Full of surprises, this human. She was unlike anything

he could have imagined.

He laid her down on the plush pillows, her expression one of shock mixed with feverish anticipation. "I'm sorry, I don't know what came over me," she stammered.

Despite her initial protest, she embraced him again, running her hands over his shoulders and chest, down the trail of dark hair running along his chiseled abs. "No need to be sorry. I'm at fault." Broc leaned in again, tasting the sweetness of her lips until she instinctively parted them, allowing their tongues to meet for the very first time. Their tender, yet rushed explorations progressed until Kelly's touch lost all hesitation and reluctance and seemed to become one with her own base instincts.

It seemed that she didn't notice, or didn't care when he slipped the soft fabric of her nightgown off her shoulders, exposing more of her ivory skin. He could resist her no more, letting his hands explore the generous curves on her body which had enticed him from the beginning. All the women Broc had grown up with and lived amongst were hardened by battle, strong and capable fighters, just like the men. There was nothing soft or gentle about their bodies. He'd never thought about it before, but from the moment he'd seen Kelly, he knew he had been missing something.

By the way she moved against him, he could tell she was strong too, for a human. But she was also delicate, irresistibly fragile. Every fiber in his body was alerted to the fact that her safety and her happiness were now to be his first priority. He would protect her from harm, and do his best to give her anything she desired. At this moment, as he laid her down on her back, allowing her fiery red hair to fan out on his bed, he knew that she desired pleasure.

He climbed on top of her, taking care not to hurt her with his considerable bulk, and continued to kiss his bride as if it was the only thing that mattered.

Her arms surrounded him, pulling him closer against her, signaling she was far from satisfied yet. She seemed as fascinated with his physique as he was with her, tracing the outlines of his clearly defined muscles with her fingertips, gently scratching at the bit of hair running along the center of his chest and downward.

"I've never done this," she gasped in his ear, but her tone made it sound more like an invitation than a protest. "That's fine, my darling, let me show you," Broc responded.

There was much he still had to show her, but tonight he focused only on one thing. The secrets he continued to hide from her; they could wait.

He tore her nightgown open all the way, once again marveling at the extent of her beauty. Her soft curves demanded to be touched, to be worshipped by Broc's lips. And so he did just that.

They caressed, licked, tasted and loved each other's bodies until the first light of dawn made an appearance through the narrow window above the bed. They gave in to all their desires but one: the first time they'd let their bodies merge would be as tradition required it.

Once they were wed.

CHAPTER SEVEN

————◆————

When Kelly finally awoke the next day, she found herself once again in the same room where she'd slept the first night. Somehow after all their illicit activity at night, Broc had mustered the effort to carry her back into her own chambers so she could rest late into the morning.

She stretched herself, finding her neck and parts of her shoulder inexplicably knotted and sore. By the time she got up, finding that she was indeed wearing the same nightgown again that had at some point been discarded on the floor in Broc's room, she couldn't help herself and let out a giggle, while wrapping her arms around herself.

But her visit to his room had left its mark; the gown wasn't quite the same anymore. In the heat of the moment, it had become torn at the neckline.

So this was what it felt like, to commit sin. But it hadn't made her feel weak and wicked, instead she felt powerful and re-energized. Perhaps her transition wouldn't be as bad as Broc had made it sound yesterday.

Kelly's night with Broc had been the stuff dreams were made of. Even though she had told herself at the start that she only intended to speak with him in his room, her mind was quickly changed by the half-naked giant she'd found after opening his door.

Never before had she seen a man whose body was so powerful and strong, yet who showed so much tenderness towards her. Some of the boys of her village had made attempts in private. They had teased and tried to tempt her, but she had never been interested.

She had never felt attracted to a man before.

And what a man he was.

Shortly after she sat up in the bed, her mind still reeling from the memories of their encounter, there was a knock on the door.

"Enter," Kelly said, in a tone that was surprisingly firm.

After the good old click-and-creak of the door, Bree appeared with breakfast and some leather strapped boots and other items she wasn't quite familiar with.

"Had a good rest?" Bree asked.

Kelly nodded, her face turning bright red in the process.

Bree squinted and gave her a long, good look, before letting her eyes rest on the torn seams of the night gown.

"I see," she said, and put the breakfast down on the table next to the bed.

Kelly's heart started to race with nerves as she waited for a comment or perhaps even a lecture.

"I've been requested to help you with these." Bree held up the boots, and something that looked like a brown leather bodice, with buckles and straps along the sides.

It seemed she was content to just ignore the evidence of Kelly's indiscretion. Did she not disapprove?

Kelly took a deep breath in the hopes it would get her nerves under control. "What are they?"

"The kind of attire needed to leave these walls," Bree clarified, without clarifying anything much.

Kelly decided not to question it, as her stomach had started to growl uncontrollably, so she focused on breakfast first. Perhaps food would help her ignore the aches she'd woken up with.

Bree busied herself with organizing the large wardrobe as Kelly ate, even though there hadn't been much time for things to get out of place. Perhaps Bree just enjoyed taking care of others. Kelly could understand, her mother had enjoyed that kind of thing too when she was still alive.

"Perhaps you would like to try this one," Bree suggested, after Kelly had finished her last bite and put the plate back down.

Kelly looked up to find her holding a dress much shorter and narrower than the gowns she was used to wearing at home. It also had a lace-up back, meaning it would be quite tightly fitted.

"Is that what those—" Kelly nodded at the leathers while speaking, "go with?"

"Indeed."

Although she wasn't quite certain she was ready to wear something so revealing, it did occur to her that a lot of the giant women at the feast had been wearing fairly similar dresses. In her village, a girl would be branded a harlot for less.

Then again, she wasn't in her village anymore. And last night's visit to Broc's room had been a lot more sinful than simply wearing a shorter dress. Kelly shrugged and nodded at Bree in agreement.

"I also thought you might want to take a bath first," Bree suggested in a tone that told Kelly this was yet another done thing on Black Isle. Fresh water was such a precious commodity on the mainland that Kelly had scarcely been afforded the opportunity to bathe every other week, and it had only been about four days since the last time.

Still, if she was going to fit into this place, she'd better behave like everyone else. Kelly didn't argue and followed Bree through a door off to the right of the large wardrobe, in that part of her room that was mostly too dark to see properly. She hadn't even noticed a doorway there before.

Of course she hadn't spent enough time in her room to properly explore it. A memory of the reasons why tickled her, making her smile as she walked through the hidden corridor, into a large square washroom.

Here the stone floor felt inexplicably warmer than in her bedroom, and the walls were adorned with glass shelves laden with strange little bottles in all shapes and colors. Kelly's eye was drawn to the door opposite to the entrance she and Bree had just come in from, which was opened to just a crack.

While Bree prepared her bath, Kelly decided to warm

herself by the fire pit in the corner and just observe. After filling water from a hanging metal tube into the large kettle shaped tub in the middle of the room, Bree collected a bucket full of glowing coals from the fire and placed them underneath. Clearly this was going to be a bath unlike any she'd ever experienced.

As they waited for the coals to do their job, Bree kept stealing glances in Kelly's direction until finally, Kelly caught on.

"What?"

"Oh I… I probably shouldn't pry. But those bruises on your neck…"

Kelly instinctively touched her neck where it still felt a little sore. How had this happened? Again, her lingering embarrassment about the previous night flared up.

Bree let out a laugh, which echoed against the stone walls of the room, making it sound even louder and deeper than normal.

"Don't be ashamed. You are to be wed, it's expected."

Kelly was well on her way to turning a deep crimson, not just on her cheeks but her ears as well. It had been a lot easier giving in to him than should have been the case. And she didn't intend for it to be discovered. She started to wonder if maybe the villagers, blaming her for her mother's death, had been right and there was something inherently wicked about her.

"We… Oh dear. I didn't realize I was bruised!"

"It will fade."

"How soon?"

"A few days perhaps, it depends. Humans heal slower, apparently." Bree still could hardly contain her amusement at Kelly's predicament. The tall female's smile was so contagious it didn't take long for Kelly to calm down as well.

"You say it's expected? Not where I come from." Kelly looked down at the coals, which were now covered with a sheath of white ash.

"No? Tell me." Bree stopped smiling, instead looking at Kelly with large, curious eyes.

It took around half an hour for the bath water to come up to a temperature Bree deemed acceptable, during which Kelly did her best to tell tales of her home. Of the rules, the way the villagers, including her father, treated their women, even of the observations she had made at the feast, where it seemed that everyone was more equal here.

By the end Kelly had Bree shaking her head.

"And they call us barbarians."

That last remark finally made Kelly smile wide, and she wondered if perhaps the giants ought to take girls from the mainland more often. Being stuck on this island didn't seem like such a bad thing after all.

Bree held out her hand, gesturing at Kelly to hand over the torn nightgown. Apparently she planned to stay while Kelly soaked in the warm water. She held back any protests about undressing in front of someone else, and took a deep breath before letting the soft, silky fabric fall down her shoulders and over her hips.

Although the female giant didn't say a word, Kelly felt her eyes darting back and forth between her, and the dress, as if she was trying not to look but couldn't help herself. Kelly awkwardly hurried into the tub, keen to be a little less exposed. The only other person to ever see her as she bathed had been her mother, and back then she'd only been a child.

As Kelly's body was enveloped by the warm water, she couldn't believe how wonderful it felt. Bathing had always been a necessary evil, and not very enjoyable during the colder times of year. Bree gathered up one of the glass bottles and returned to the tub, trickling a bit of the liquid into the water until the whole room was filled with the sweet fragrance of a summer meadow. It was magic.

Kelly closed her eyes, enjoying how her muscles—even her bruised neck—completely relaxed. Her thoughts travelled back to last night; how Broc had made her feel when he touched her so intimately. How everything she thought she knew about right and wrong suddenly seemed to fade until it no longer mattered. She wasn't in her village anymore. The rules of her people no longer applied.

Even though she knew Bree was still around, Kelly couldn't help but take some time floating like that with her eyes shut, thinking through everything that had happened so far. Only yesterday she had been focused on escaping at the first opportunity. But now, things didn't seem so clear cut anymore. The magnetic pull Broc had over her made her feel like becoming his wife was not so bad after all. Life in the castle seemed pleasant enough as well.

Today she was going to explore the rest of the island apparently, hence the boots. Kelly no longer felt the urge to run, but a little voice in her head still pressed her to keep the option to escape open, should she need it.

———◆———

"Whenever you're ready," a gruff female voice dragged Kelly out of her deep thoughts. She opened her eyes, blinking a few times to stop the damp steam from her bath from clouding her vision. Rhea.

"I'll ensure she gets dressed," Bree said. If Kelly had been uncomfortable getting into the tub in front of Bree earlier, she definitely didn't want to get out with Rhea watching now. Kelly shifted awkwardly in the water, looking around the room for something—anything—that would afford her some coverage. The tall blonde warrior had her arm propped up on her hip and kept staring down at Kelly.

She did not seem in a mood to leave.

Bree seemed to sense Kelly's discomfort and intervened. "Rhea, I said I'll ensure she gets ready shortly." Reluctantly, Rhea turned away from Kelly to face Bree, and shrugged her shoulders.

"Fine. Get her to the drawbridge in ten minutes." Rhea turned on her heel without even shooting another glance in Kelly's direction and vanished, pulling the door shut behind her with a loud thump.

"She doesn't like me," Kelly mumbled.

"Rhea can be peculiar. But she's not a bad person." Bree smiled at Kelly, but it didn't do much to reassure her. "Let's get you ready so we don't make her wait unnecessarily."

When Bree had come into her bedroom earlier, Kelly had hoped she was going to go out and explore the island with Broc, but as it turned out, she was to be accompanied by Rhea. Disappointing as it was, she tried not to let it show.

Bree handed her a large, soft cloth, and Kelly did her best to dry herself off without showing too much skin. Her shoulder felt a lot better after the bath, but the hot water had turned her entire body from a pale ivory to bright pink, making her feel even more vulnerable than before. Bree meanwhile brought in some alien looking undergarments, which Kelly clumsily put on, before they returned to the bedroom where the dress and leathers were.

It really was a rather short dress, unlike anything Kelly had ever worn even as a little girl. Even on top, she felt quite exposed, the deep neckline revealing a bit of cleavage, further accentuated by the tight bodice which Bree had expertly laced up from the back. Next, she put on the boots, which fit surprisingly well due to the many fasteners and buckles.

Next, Bree helped her put on even more leather over the dress, harder than that of her boots, as if it was meant to be some kind of protective plate covering her torso. A dark woolen cloak was to be worn on top as soon as she'd leave the castle. You never knew when the weather would turn during this time in early spring and it seemed much colder out here than on the mainland.

Kelly again wished she had a mirror, because looking down at herself, all she could see was bare skin. She felt ridiculous, but again kept her concerns to herself. The second Bree deemed her ready, after braiding her damp hair and pinning it upwards, she led Kelly through the door and down the various confusing corridors to where Rhea was waiting. The Drawbridge.

CHAPTER EIGHT

———◆———

When Broc entered the large hall that only hours earlier had hosted the beginning of the Reaping feast, a small group of notable persons had already assembled. There was Teaq, of course, who had called the meeting, along with his right-hand man and commander of Black Isle's fleet of ships.

Then there were three elders; ankle length robes matched the pale grey of their thinning hair. The Black Isle way of life meant that surviving into old age was a luxury not afforded to many. When an islander reached a certain, ripe age, he either sailed off into the twilight or cast off his armor and weapons and dedicated himself to the study of their history and culture. Elders served as librarians, as advisors to the king and as developers of military strategy.

Yorrick, second in command of the castle guard, was present, though his superior, Rhea, was not.

So, nearly everyone who held an important position in his court was in attendance. Perhaps Rhea had better things to do this morning.

"Settle down, everyone!" As usual, Broc did not need to raise his voice much. The small group did indeed quieten down quickly and everyone found a seat.

The last one standing was Teaq, who held his position beside the entrance to the hall, with his arms crossed.

"Let us begin," Broc spoke up again, then turned to face Teaq. "Why are we here?"

Teaq cleared his throat. "The threat from the north is growing. We must prepare for war."

Broc frowned.

"Is there any particular reason for your suspicions?"

"The prophecy determines it, my king," one of the elders said.

Broc pressed his lips together. He did not rule based on guesswork and so-called prophecies. Stories and legends, that's all they were. Useful to learn from, in order to avoid making the same mistakes, but far from a roadmap for the future.

"There is something not right with the girl," Teaq said.

Broc felt the hairs on the back of his neck stand up. His patience for Teaq's growing paranoia was wearing thin.

Still, he composed himself before responding. "What exactly do you mean?"

"Call it instinct." Teaq straightened himself. "Something in her mannerisms. In her behavior. Remember I am more intuitive when it comes to reading body language. Benefits of my wolf lineage."

"It's all in the prophecy," the same white-haired man who had spoken a moment ago piped up again.

Broc shook his head. "Would you prefer if she spent her first days here, cowering in a corner, mourning the loss of everything she had known so far in life? Everyone's transition is different. The last one suffered exceptionally.

We've already taken steps to avoid a repeat of the same, and when clearly our new approach is working, you want to call it evidence of something—I'm not even sure of what."

Teaq glared at him. His brother wasn't accustomed to having his judgement questioned.

Then again, neither was Broc.

The two of them stared each other down for an awkward several seconds.

"I just want to make sure you know what you're doing. That you have thought things through," Teaq all but growled.

"We need fresh blood. That's not up for debate, just ask the Elders. And whether anyone here likes it or not, I need an heir."

"You seem to be liking it just fine in this case," Teaq mumbled.

"What? Speak up, so the entire council can hear," Broc warned.

"The girl has had an effect on you since the moment we collected her from the mainland."

Broc closed his eyes and inhaled deeply. His patience really was running out. Kelly was a beautiful woman, a fact he had noticed from the start. So what? He was king. Was he not deserving of a beautiful mate?

Had Teaq wanted her for himself? Was all this just jealousy on Teaq's part?

"An effect, you say. Is this all just preparation for a challenge? Let me know right now, so we can settle it."

"I just want what's best for our people," Teaq explained.

Broc raised an eyebrow. "What's best for our people is to have a stable rule, a royal union and hopefully soon after, an heir to the throne."

"You've made up your mind then. That you'll make her your queen," Teaq said.

Broc straightened his shoulders. "It is time we had a queen, don't you think? And the rules forbid me from taking one of our own as my mate."

"And I suppose you've had a taste as well. I can practically smell it on you."

Anger flared up in Broc's chest. "What of it? No rules were broken."

"What of the coming war?" one of the other elders interrupted.

Clearly it was only Teaq who was interested in dragging Broc's private affairs into this council meeting.

Broc forced his attention away from his brother. "What coming war? Do we have any proof of what's coming?"

"The prophecy…"

Broc sighed. "Fine. What does the prophecy say?"

"That during a time of great change, two moons before the summer solstice, a stranger arrives among our people who hides a terrible secret. a power that could win or lose wars, one that could destroy us or mean our salvation.

That this stranger's arrival brings with it the third great age of war as our enemies try to win this power for themselves."

Vague, as prophecies usually were. How convenient. Although he'd never voice these suspicions aloud, Broc had long wondered if the old scrolls contained so many riddles and vague language to keep the Elders busy during times of relative peace. One could debate for days about what a particular passage meant as everyone usually had a slightly different interpretation.

"And you're thinking the human is the stranger mentioned in the prophecy?" Broc asked.

"Who else?" The Elders had spoken in unison. So they were actually in agreement about something for a change.

"And her power?" Broc asked.

The Elders exchanged some looks among themselves. "We have some ideas, but we will find out for sure what it is only once it is too late," one said.

"So in short, there really is nothing we can do, except bar all *strangers* from the island. Something which we cannot afford at this moment in time, when we still need our arrangement with the humans to add some much needed variety to our blood line," Broc concluded. "Or is your advice to stop the Reaping ritual in its entirety?"

The Elders were silent for a moment. "Not exactly. The Reaping ritual is essential to our survival. We are not even certain the outcome of the prophecy can be affected as such. But we need to be aware and fortify our position nonetheless. The events leading up to the third age of war are set in stone. However, the outcome of the war is not yet foretold."

The Elders' position seemed a lot more nuanced than Broc had given them credit for. He nodded. "Very well. I see nothing wrong with being prepared for any and all eventualities."

"We should keep an eye on the human though," Teaq butted in.

"To what effect?"

"To learn of her powers, before anyone else does, of course!"

If she even has any powers. The notion that this innocent young woman hid a terrible secret was ludicrous. Her only power, as far as Broc could see, was her sense of reasoning and a certain level of intelligence which was sadly lacking in his current company.

As well as an amazing appetite for pleasure. The memories of last night lingered on Broc's mind.

"I ordered Rhea to take her out onto the plateau, to assess her fighting skills," Teaq added.

That explained why Rhea wasn't here this morning. The two of them were in on it together.

Broc slowly shook his head. He had been king for seven years now. Teaq hadn't liked it, but he had won the crown fair and square. Broc had always aimed to be a fair ruler; to listen to his people, and never let his emotions meddle in official business. This morning, things were not so clear cut.

He found it difficult to not let his feelings about Kelly influence the way he handled this latest development.

It was a load of rubbish, though. If you read through the old scrolls long enough, you'd find a prophecy or prediction for everything under the sun. Had the Elders really come up with this on their own, or had Teaq tasked them to look for something specific to fit his agenda?

And what had really sparked his paranoia about brewing wars and dangerous invaders into Black Isle territory? There had to be something more to this particular story.

Perhaps the explanation was as simple as Teaq finally losing his mind.

Broc had to find out what exactly was going on within these walls, but first he would make sure he'd get to know Kelly a bit more. His own instincts weren't usually so bad either, no matter what Teaq thought. Surely, if the human had any ill intent, he would have picked up on it by now.

"Regardless of what you and Rhea have come up with together, the transition is going ahead as planned. I expect that arrangements are made so that I may announce my intended union with Kelly Chaslain of West Hythe by the next full moon."

Teaq shook his head. "As you wish, but I—"

"It's not up for discussion," Broc interrupted. "You

heard the Elders. The events foretold in the prophecy cannot be stopped, so there's no point in trying. We *will*, however, prepare ourselves for the next great war. Build up our armory. Strengthen our castle walls. Test the war horns on all the Isles."

He turned to address the Elders. "If there is anything in our records to help us fight the Sea Folk… I don't have to tell you how helpful that would be."

"Yes, my king," the Elders spoke in unison. "We will read on it."

Broc finally turned to face Yorrick, who had stood by in silence, watching the entire argument with a pained expression on his face. It seemed obvious that this situation had been spearheaded by Teaq and Rhea, and Yorrick was just an innocent bystander, so Broc diverted his attention away from him again.

"And as we're preparing for a possible siege, I would suggest you, Teaq, take a group of our best hunters to the mainland to gather supplies. The Reaping Feast is continuing regardless, but it would be unwise to be left without any reserves after."

CHAPTER NINE

"Let's go," Rhea snapped, and signaled towards the guards to open the large gate. The huge wood and metal structure creaked into action, and soon they were able to walk out of the castle and onto the bridge.

Kelly was glad to have the woolen cloak, because the island was still being battered by freezing winds. Rhea, who was just wearing a short dress with a similar leather breastplate, didn't seem to mind the weather at all, and marched straight down the path carved out between the rocky mountain faces, heading towards the harbor hidden in between the cliffs.

Nobody could ever guess this was here, Kelly thought as she looked around. All one would be able to make out from the sea was the angular facade of the fortified castle, but the color of it matched the surrounding rocks so perfectly that it would be difficult for any human to distinguish from afar. The harbor was so completely surrounded by cliffs and spiky rocks, not only was it extremely well hidden, it would also be quite treacherous to sail in and out of.

"Are these all the ships or are there more?" Kelly asked, but immediately regretted it when Rhea gave her a foul look.

"What do you know of combat? Broc asked me to assess you, because any woman of Black Isle must be able to defend herself in battle." Rhea folded her arms as she waited for her answer.

This was a surprise. So they weren't exploring the island at all, but Kelly was meant to *fight?*

"Not much. On the mainland, women don't fight." Rhea scoffed and shook her head slowly, the disgust evident on her face.

"That does not surprise me. No problem, I'm supposed to teach you, follow me." Rhea turned around as quickly as she had initially stopped for her brief interrogation. Kelly just did her best, trying to keep up with the leggy female giant as she marched up the slight incline leading around the harbor, towards a door set into the mountainous rock.

"Wait here," Rhea barked, as she took a key from a little pouch on her belt and removed the lock from the heavy, weather damaged door.

Kelly observed her as she disappeared into the dark cavern beyond the door, reappearing shortly with two rather large sword-shaped pieces of wood as well as two metal weapons of a similar shape and size.

Mother, help me.

Kelly eyed the weapons glumly but tried not to let her apprehensions show. These were a lot bigger and heavier looking than the sticks she and Ferris had play-fought with when they were younger. At the time she had been able to keep up with most of the village boys in similar sparring games, but Rhea was a much more intimidating opponent.

"Follow me," Rhea said, marching back down the path, around the harbor, and up some winding stone steps leading higher up into the mountainous center of the island.

They hiked for a while, at least an hour at what was a brisk pace for Kelly, with not a word said between the two of them.

How long would this go on for? How would she have energy to spar with Rhea after such a long hike? By the end of it, they reached some kind of plateau, only partially screened off from the land below by low shrubs and the occasional tree that had clung on to the otherwise rocky ground. The landscape lower down was also mainly stony, except for a few patches of greenery which surrounded a couple of small huts that clung to the hillside. After seeing nothing but black stone ever since arriving on the island, Kelly felt a surge of excitement at the small glimpse of familiarity ahead of her. Although slightly different in style, the huts looked vaguely similar to the farm buildings used in her village.

Other than that, there was nothing of note in the landscape that Kelly could see. Just more sharp looking rocks and peaks, and just a small patch of pine trees lower down towards the shore. The waters surrounding the island looked as hostile and untamed as the sea in front of the castle, and spiky rocks stuck out of the surface all around the perimeter. There was no way one could swim to the mainland from here; anyone stupid enough to try would be smashed to death against one of those cliffs. After a few moments catching her breath, Kelly noticed that Rhea had been staring at her.

"It's quite different from the mainland, isn't it?" Rhea asked.

"A bit."

"You know before your people turned on us, we didn't have to live in this miserable place." Rhea's bitterness shone through in her tone, as she almost spat out her words.

Kelly reminded herself of Bree's words, that Rhea wasn't a bad person. That was why Rhea was angry, she felt the humans had taken her home away, no matter how long ago.

"We lived in peace, and then your King Edrick came over the No Man's Range to the south and burnt down our villages in order to take the mainland for himself." King Edrick, Kelly had heard of him in some of the ancient tales. The village elders had spoken of him like a great and fearsome warrior, who had banished all evil from the northern lands, making them a safe place for mankind to live.

"I didn't know…" Kelly stammered, not wanting to upset the female fighter beside her, especially while she was carrying all those weapons.

"Oh, it is true. That swine came and tricked us before he murdered our children and raped our women. At the same time the Sea Folk attacked from the water and we were overrun. The only way we could survive was by coming   here."

"And the treaty?" Kelly asked. The treaty that everyone in the villages on the mainland was so disapproving of, the one that meant sacrificing a young girl—Kelly in this case—to keep the peace.

"That. That came after. The elders of the Hythe approached our king at the time, Nerys, one winter many years ago. They proposed an exchange, they'd choose one of their kin every eight years as an offering to our clan, in exchange for protection from the dangers that lie further out to sea." Rhea stared darkly at the waters that lay beyond the shoreline.

"I don't know why he ever agreed to it. He should have insisted on a safe haven for our people on the mainland, rather than fight to protect the cowards who put us here. Instead he accepted their terms."

Kelly was taken aback by Rhea's story. The events of the Great War between humans and giants had been a popular tale to tell at the occasional village feast. Only in the version of her childhood, King Edrick was a hero, and the giants were a fearsome evil needing to be wiped from this earth. The proper story she knew did not feature any enemy from the seas beyond the Black Isles. And the so-called Sea Folk, people who lived underneath the seas, were rejected as myth by most, including her father.

But what did she know. She'd only been on this island for a couple of days.

And before that, Kelly herself had been wondering if even the giants were only a myth. After all, no one in her village had ever seen a live giant before and lived to tell the tale.

Could it be that there are other strange beings out there? Right now, looking at the strange landscape surrounding her, flanked by a 6 and a half foot tall woman, it seemed entirely plausible.

"Enough talk. Let's start what we came here to do." Rhea turned to face Kelly, and threw a wooden stick in her direction, which Kelly caught surprisingly easily, before putting the real swords down on a flat rock beside her. "You're holding it wrong."

Kelly looked at the positioning of Rhea's hands and tried to copy her. She was somewhat in shock that they were actually going to *fight*. She wasn't ready.

"Better, now come at me and try to stab me with it," Rhea ordered.

Hesitating for a moment, Kelly tried to tighten her grip on the rough wood, but a few splinters cut painfully into her palm. "It's broken," she protested.

"It's broken," Rhea copied Kelly's tone and let out a loud, disingenuous laugh. "Try telling your enemy that in the middle of a battle."

When am I *ever going to be in a battle with anyone?* Kelly thought.

Rather than wait for Kelly to make a move, Rhea charged in her direction with her wooden sword held high up in the air. Kelly instinctively stepped aside, dodging Rhea's attack, then indeed tried to stab her, only to have her stick swatted away and out of her hand, clattering onto the ground several feet away from the two women.

Kelly was shaking and sweat broke through her cold skin.

"Now do it again."

Although the walk up the mountainside and back down again had tired her out quite a bit, Kelly rubbed her wrist, which ached from the impact of Rhea's disarming blow, and picked up her practice sword again.

Mother, give me strength!

She did not last much longer in the second round. Or the third, or fourth.

Throughout the practice session with Rhea, Kelly felt in conflict with herself and her upbringing. This wasn't the game she had played with Ferris when they were young.

If her father could see what she was doing, learning how to *properly* fight with a sword, he would drop dead of shock. At the same time, she understood that this was the way things were in this new world. Perhaps if she tried her best to grasp at least the basics of the training Rhea was trying to give her, Broc would be proud of her.

That was her main motivator now.

Only yesterday she might have considered how this training might help her escape this place. Now, she kept on catching herself wondering what it would be like to become Broc's bride.

In a very short two days, Kelly had completely changed her outlook.

After numerous rounds, during which Rhea managed to knock the wooden stick out of Kelly's hand every single time, they paused for a while. They sat down on the flatter rocks towards the edge of the plateau on which they stood and rested in silence. Despite the winds still battering the island from seemingly all sides, Kelly felt warm enough to remove her cloak.

Kelly remembered some of the things Broc had told her. About how hard life on these islands was. Seeing the scenery out here drove things home for her.

How did one feed so many hungry giants, when there was no land here suitable for farming?

Except for some seagulls circling the skies, Kelly hadn't seen a single animal on the way over here. No sheep; not even any chickens or rabbits.

And yet at the feast, they'd enjoyed a wealth of foods. They didn't trade with the mainland, except for the Reaping. And if these so-called Sea Folk kept on attacking them, they probably didn't trade with them either.

So where had all the meat come from?

Her curiosity was sparked yet again, but looking at

Rhea's grim expression, Kelly kept her questions to herself. Perhaps she'd get the chance to ask Broc about all this.

If indeed she was going to stay here, she might as well understand this place and its people better.

CHAPTER TEN

———◆———

They ate, they drank, they made merry. The second
night of the Reaping feast had gone by much like
the first.

Broc admired the way Kelly carried herself. She was
adjusting.

Even the long day of training with Rhea hadn't
dampened her spirits.

"Everything is fine, isn't it? I mean, *you* are fine?" Broc
had asked her when he first saw her, just to reassure
himself. A day alone with Rhea… that could have gone
any number of ways.

She had smiled and placed her hand on his briefly.

"I am," she'd said, before elaborating in a more playful
tone. "Better now to be sitting here with you."

Now, as he looked down on her, naked and fast asleep
in his bed, he could see that perhaps she had underplayed
things a little.

She'd had a hard day. These marks on her arms and
legs hadn't been there before. Red grazes covered her
lower arms and her knees, down to her shins. They weren't
deep, but they stood out starkly against her ivory skin.

His kind healed so fast, he'd never seen anything like it
before. It stung, to see her this way.

Although she'd shown the same enthusiasm, the same

passion as the night before, her touch had changed. She wasn't as free in her movements. Had she been in pain?

He would ask her, except he didn't have the heart to wake her up. She so very clearly needed the rest.

If Teaq and Rhea's plan had gone too far, there would be repercussions.

Everyone on the island had undergone a certain amount of combat training. But this was different. Kelly was to be his queen.

He'd fight to the death to keep her from harm. She would never have to pick up a sword in battle herself; he would make sure of it.

As he continued to observe her, how innocently she lay there, he couldn't help but wonder about the things Teaq and the Elders had said during the Council meeting. Surely *he* was the one keeping secrets in this room, not Kelly.

This prophecy the Elders had dug up; either it was simply a misinterpretation, or there was someone else; some other outsider whom they all ought to worry about.

It certainly couldn't be Kelly. Not his queen.

She stirred and turned onto her side, moaning softly in the process.

"What is it, my darling?" Broc whispered.

He sat down beside her and gently rested his hand on her bare shoulder.

She sighed.

"Mother. Why have you forsaken me?" Kelly

demanded.

Broc frowned. Her eyes remained closed. A dream, perhaps? Or a memory.

"Nobody has forsaken you. You're not alone."

Despite his attempt to comfort her, she grew more restless, turning onto her back again and shaking her head vigorously.

"I don't understand. Why did have to you leave us?"

Clearly there was something eating away at her. Broc regretted not asking Kelly about her past and her family some more. That might have afforded him some insights now.

Broc lay down beside her, wrapping his arm around her and pulling her body against his.

This seemed to help. Kelly's breaths became deeper and more regular. Her formerly tense expression relaxed.

"You're safe now," Broc whispered in her ear.

"Mhmm."

"Sleep on." He rested his head on the pillow beside hers.

This was how they remained, side by side, until shortly before dawn. Broc gathered her up in a sheet, ever careful not to wake her, and carried her back to her own room. He paused for a moment, watching as she settled into her new position.

He couldn't explain it. How Kelly had awoken all these feelings in him.

It was his duty as king to take care of all his subjects,

obviously. And as his future queen, Kelly held a special position. But this wasn't about duty. It was about instinct.

Remembering the scars on her otherwise flawless skin, Broc balled his fists.

He wouldn't stand idly by as Rhea and Teaq conspired to make Kelly's life unnecessarily difficult.

But his responsibilities took him away from her most of the day. He needed an ally. Someone he could trust to be truthful with him, but who could move around the island unnoticed.

As he closed the heavy door to Kelly's room as quietly as he could, a shadow in the corner of his eye attracted his attention. Her scent was unmistakably familiar.

"Bree?" Broc called out.

The young woman appeared from around the corner. Her head bowed as a sign of respect. She'd always been a bit timid around him, but he trusted her. That was why he had assigned her to take care of Kelly during the transition. She was a born protector.

Who better to help him with his latest problem?

"There's something we must discuss," Broc started.

Bree raised her head and met his gaze. "Anything, my king."

"It's about Kelly…"

At the mention of her name, Bree's eyes lit up. It was obvious that the woman had developed a certain fondness for his future bride. Broc smiled. Bree was the perfect ally indeed.

"I would like you to make sure that nothing untoward happens to her. The training with Rhea is fine and well, but Rhea has never trained a human before. Their bodies... they work differently from ours."

Bree eyes darted back at Kelly's room, then lingered on him again. "She's fragile."

"She heals more slowly," Broc clarified.

"You'd like me to accompany them. Watch over her."

Broc nodded. "But it cannot be obvious. Use your powers. Stay out of sight."

Bree opened her mouth as if to protest, but kept quiet when another dark figure approached the two of them in the corridor.

"Up so early?" Teaq asked.

"There is much to do," Broc said.

He exchanged one last look and a subtle nod with Bree, who quickly turned around and made herself scarce. The woman had never been too fond of Teaq, whose gruff and direct nature was indeed something of an acquired taste.

"This is hardly the time, brother," Teaq remarked while nodding sideways at Kelly's door.

"Oh, no, I was on the way to the Watch Point," Broc explained.

"In your night clothes?" Teaq argued.

"I had a feeling. An instinct. We cannot afford complacency."

"Finally something we both can agree on."

The two brothers exchanged a long look. Teaq had immediately steered the conversation to Broc's presence in the corridor. But what was *he* up to so early in the morning? More conspiring and scheming, perhaps?

"Perhaps we could inspect the fortifications on the Eastern Isle today. The weather seems good for it." Teaq folded his arms in front of his chest.

"Very well. It has been a while since I've visited those parts."

Was Teaq actively trying to get Broc off the main island today? Refusing would only raise suspicions though. With Bree firmly on his and Kelly's side, Broc felt it safe to play along.

"We can join the morning patrol," Teaq said.

Broc nodded. "I'll be there."

Rather than go back to his room, he turned in the opposite direction and soon found his way to the Watch Point, just as he'd told Teaq. It was where he liked to come and think.

With everything that had been happening, he had a lot to mull over.

But as the cold sea winds hit his face, forcing him to close his eyes for a moment, there was only one thing on his mind: Kelly.

———— ◆ ————

"This part of the island has always been more vulnerable.

It's too remote. We need more guards here." Broc gestured at the wall surrounding the barren wilderness of the island before them. Then he turned to face Teaq, who had folded his arms.

"More guards. When the invasion comes, a few extra guards aren't going to help us." Teaq had to speak up to make himself heard over the strong sea winds. The boat they had sailed on from the main island was being thrown around vigorously on the waves surrounding the island.

"What would you advise, then?" Broc asked. His elder brother could be quite the know-it-all, but he did have a keen instinct when it came to military strategy.

"We need a better method for the guards already stationed here to signal in case of enemy sightings."

"Another lighthouse?" Broc asked, glancing over at the lone tower toward the westernmost point of the island.

"Perhaps." Teaq was acting unlike his usual self. His expression was thoughtful, and he was even more tight-lipped than normal. Had the prospect of war spooked him? Or was it something else?

Broc would have to find out.

"We should convene regular meetings with the Elders. Perhaps they have ideas that might help," Broc suggested.

Teaq nodded in silence.

For a moment, the two brothers stood quietly by the railing of the ship, still staring at the island. This was the land their father had left them. Now it was up to them to defend it from the enemies that surrounded them.

It wasn't a light burden to bear, the responsibility to keep all the islanders safe. But who else was there to carry it?

Broc sighed and closed his eyes. The salty air had a way of cleansing one's thoughts, just like he had attempted to do earlier on the Watch Point at the castle.

His thoughts were far from clean, though. They kept on returning to the illicit activities of the previous night, no matter how hard he tried to focus.

He glanced over at Teaq. Luckily Broc's thoughts were his own.

Even so, these emotions, they weren't a sign of weakness, were they? They felt like a powerful force, one that would enable him to move mountains if he had to.

He'd conquer worlds for her.

And when the time came, he would find a way to defeat Black Isle's enemies to keep her safe. If it was the last thing he did.

"We should go on land. Speak with the guards. See what we can learn that may help."

Broc turned to look at his brother again, but Teaq seemed distracted again. What on earth was going on with him? Was he jealous of Broc's newfound happiness, perhaps? If Broc didn't know any better, he might have thought it was time for him to find a bride of his own. Was that why he was trying to meddle in Broc's relationship with Kelly? Had jealousy inspired him to attempt to undermine her?

"Brother, did you hear me?" Broc asked.

"Yes… Yes, of course. I have some errands to run on the island as it is. I'll join you in the main watch tower once I am done."

Broc shrugged, but scrutinized Teaq's face for a moment longer. "Very well then."

Errands… It wasn't in his nature to make excuses, and yet Teaq was being uncharacteristically vague. So many secrets all of a sudden.

What on earth was Teaq up to on this remote and barren island in the sea?

CHAPTER ELEVEN

Another morning, another day of training with Rhea. Kelly followed Rhea along the now somewhat familiar path across the drawbridge and up the hillside until they were once more on the plateau where they had trained the day before.

She was no weakling, but she was no giant either. Her body was still recovering from all the unfamiliar movements Rhea had taught her.

The stiffness she'd felt after waking this morning hadn't worn off yet. The walk had only made her muscles protest even more.

And her right arm. It felt like lead.

"Here, take it," Rhea ordered while handing Kelly the real sword.

"What? No, I'm not ready," she protested.

Rhea just glared at her. Clearly the female giant was in no mood to argue.

Kelly's palm burned when she closed her fingers around the handle of sword. Small blisters had started to form at the base of each of her digits. Her wrist still burned from the repeated impacts she had received each time Rhea had disarmed her.

She looked down at her weapon; crude and not very sharp. The blade had developed a bit of rust on one side.

It wasn't in the best shape, much like Kelly herself.

"Can't we train with the wooden ones again? It's only been a day."

"And tomorrow, we might all be dead. You'd better learn more quickly," Rea grumbled.

It wasn't that Kelly didn't *want* to learn. She did. She wanted to make Broc proud, after all.

But she wasn't as strong, and certainly not as experienced.

Oh, Mother. What do I do?

"Well? Are you just going to stand there? You're not going to cry, are you?" Rhea said.

Kelly bit her bottom lip. No, she was not. She wouldn't give her the pleasure of breaking down now.

Give me strength.

Kelly closed her eyes and inhaled deeply.

"So, attack me, then!" Rhea demanded.

Kelly raised her weapon high into the air just as Rhea had shown her previously, and charged as fast as her aching legs could carry her.

Rhea dodged her attack, prompting Kelly to turn on her heel and swing the sword downward. Yet another move they had practiced the previous day. She almost grazed Rhea's arm, but the latter stepped aside and raised her own weapon, bringing it down hard. Sparks flew as the two blades connected.

The impact was much harsher than what Kelly had expected from their previous session. She dropped the sword and grabbed her wrist.

"Bloody hell!" Kelly shouted.

Rhea chuckled. "Best get used to the pain. The enemy won't wait for your recovery; he'll just strike you down when he has the chance."

Kelly glared at the female giant. There was no need for this. The woman had one whole foot on her. And years of training.

Mother, give me strength!

Rhea raised her blade and held its tip to Kelly's throat. "The enemy would just kill you right here."

"Are you?" Kelly asked.

"Am I what?" Rhea's tone was still full of ridicule.

"Are you my enemy?" Kelly demanded.

Rhea smirked. "I'm just supposed to train you. Whether you like the lessons or not."

"There's a difference between training and taunting. Watch yourself," Kelly hissed.

She wasn't sure if it was the pain, or a lingering effect from last night's wine-fuelled festivities that had given her ill-advised courage.

"Or what, my dear? You'll tell our dear king that I've been mean to you?"

Kelly closed her eyes and tried to focus. For whatever reason, Rhea had hated her from the start. Getting into a confrontation out here alone with her wasn't just stupid, it would serve no purpose. The only choice she had was to play Rhea's game.

She pushed the weapon away from her throat and picked up her own sword again while trying to ignore the sting the blade's edge had left on her palm.

"I'm not going to let this happen again," Kelly grumbled under her breath. "I swear it on the graves of my forefathers. On my mother's grave."

"What's that?" Rhea asked.

Kelly shook her head. "I'm ready."

Sure enough, Kelly's body felt revitalized. It was amazing what a bit of anger could achieve.

"Better be," Rhea said, before initiating the attack herself this time.

Kelly swung as hard as she could, landing a firm blow on Rhea's sword this time. The pain in her wrist was almost blinding, but she didn't flinch.

"Not bad, but not good enough!" Rhea turned and struck Kelly's weapon in return; from the bottom this time.

Kelly wasn't prepared for that. She could no longer hold on.

Mother, save me from this pain!

With her weapon once more on the ground, and Kelly holding her hurt arm tightly against her chest, a peculiar sensation came over her.

Suddenly, she found herself afloat, looking down on her own crouching form as well as Rhea, who stood by with her hand on her hip.

Kelly was no tattletale, but did Broc even know about this? He'd told her she wouldn't be harmed. Her injured wrist. Was this not also harm?

Rhea raised her sword over Kelly's defenseless form.

How easy it would be to strike this coward down where she stands. A training accident. That's what I'll say.

Kelly's anger flared up again. She didn't know how she could see what she did, and hear what she had heard. It didn't matter.

Rhea took another step forward. *Soon, you'll no longer stand in my way…*

Oh no, you don't, Kelly thought.

A vision appeared to her; red, wavy hair, a familiar face.

Darling, is this what you want? the apparition asked.

Kelly nodded. *Yes, Mother. This is what is necessary.*

The figure vanished as quickly as it had appeared. All of Kelly's energy. All her focus was aimed at only one thing: survival.

Before Rhea's sword even had the chance of coming down on top of Kelly's back, a blinding flash of light surrounded the two women and Rhea was thrown backwards over the edge of the plateau.

Kelly gasped as she was sucked into her body again. She was completely unscathed. The powerful explosion she had just observed had not affected her at all.

Not so, Rhea, whose angry snarls could be heard some way down the hillside.

What had just happened? Had she imagined it?

Kelly scampered toward the edge of the plateau and peered down. A figure lay quite some distance away; Rhea must have fallen at least fifteen feet straight down, and then rolled the rest of the way. But the female giant was in no mood to stay on her back. She scrambled onto her feet and wiped a blood-stained lock of hair out of her face.

"I'll get you for this, witch!" Rhea threatened.

Her face underwent an otherworldly change. A grimace momentarily covered in fur. Sharp teeth. A snout.

Kelly stumbled backwards in shock

First the bolt of blue light and now this.

It had to be a trick. Somehow Rhea had manipulated her; maybe she'd put poisoned mushrooms into her breakfast that had given her these strange visions. *Maybe...*

It took Rhea less than a minute to charge up the hillside. She grabbed Kelly firmly by the shoulders and glared at her. Her face was once again normal. Human-like.

Kelly couldn't help but stare.

What on earth was going on here?

"You shouldn't have shown your hand so quickly! It's all over for you now!" Rhea hissed.

Kelly didn't know how to respond. There was nothing to say. None of what had happened made any sense. And she felt so drained all of a sudden, her mind was fogging over.

"You're under arrest for witchcraft. Good luck wooing

Broc from down in the dungeons."

Of course. All this time, Rhea had been jealous. Kelly couldn't believe she hadn't seen it before. She had wanted to be queen. And then Kelly had come along and messed up all her plans.

"He'll see through this, you know. Tricking me like this," Kelly whispered.

The fatigue threatened to overwhelm, but she couldn't show weakness. Not now.

Rhea scoffed. "Tricking *you*? You're the one who has been tricking all of us. Infiltrating our walls by pretending to be some helpless human, when in fact you're a most dangerous enemy yourself. Sorceress!"

Kelly groggily shook her head. If she got a moment with Broc, she'd be able to explain it all. Rhea's jealousy. Her crazy scheme accusing Kelly of witchcraft. There was no such thing, after all.

Darling, be strong, said that familiar voice in Kelly's head.

No, she was just imagining it. Mushrooms, or some other poison. Those gave you visions that could drive grown men insane.

She couldn't allow her mind to be corrupted like that. It was all a dream. A figment of her imagination. None of this was real.

Kelly's legs threatened to buckle but Rhea had other ideas and held her upright. Once her hands were tied firmly behind her back, she was prodded and shoved into motion again.

Kelly had come full circle. A prisoner. Just like how she had started out on the shores of Hythe Bay only days ago.

She struggled to keep pace with Rhea, who began dragging her down the mountain path and back toward the castle.

Nobody would believe this crazy story, surely. There were no witches anymore. They had died out a long time ago, if they ever even existed at all.

There was no such thing as magic.

Was there?

"I don't…" Kelly tried to speak. "I'm not…"

Rhea prodded her in the back.

One foot in front of the other.

Looking down at the ground, it all seemed so alien to Kelly. These leather strapped boots Bree had given her. They might as well have been made of lead, given how difficult each passing step had become.

In the distance, the castle came into view. But Kelly could give no more.

Her legs buckled and her mind sunk into a dense fog.

Rest, my child. You'll need time to recharge and recover.

Kelly tried to respond, to argue and question this voice in her head. But she was unable to.

Far away, another voice.

Rhea, cursing.

"Coward. Witch! You'll regret making me carry you!"

That was the last Kelly could remember.

CHAPTER TWELVE

A warning horn sounded in the distance, which immediately urged the guards on the fortifications into action. Broc and Teaq also pulled their swords and ran towards the group of men converging on the lower sea wall.

"What is it?" Teaq called out.

One of the guards; his horn still in his right hand, pointed at the water's edge. Two soldiers were in the process of hauling in a large net. Within it, a figure, flailing and writhing furiously.

Broc leaned across the wall to get a better look.

Greenish, shimmery skin, and long silver hair.

Well, I'll be damned...

"It cannot be," Teaq said. His voice was uncharacteristically thin, like for once in his life something had genuinely surprised him.

Broc inhaled sharply and straightened his back. If his brother wasn't in a mood to show decorum, at least he should.

"Well, let's see it," he ordered in a firm voice.

The guards looked up briefly, then dragged the figure fully ashore. One kneeled down, restraining the sea creature in something of a strangle-hold, while the other quickly tied it up.

Then, they removed the remainder of the net and forced her up. She stopped struggling immediately as she became aware of her new surroundings.

A fully grown mermaid.

Her eyes shone golden in the subdued sunlight attempting to break through the clouds. She looked at the two men with about as much consideration as one would give a cockroach, or a fly.

"Well, you don't see *that* every day," Broc remarked.

He'd seen Sea Folk before, of course. They were stealthy, and preferred to attack mostly from underneath the water. Prisoners of war were a rare occurrence in their bloody conflict with Weiland, King of the Seas, but occasionally one had been caught.

Sea Folk soldiers were all male, though, so no one on Black Isle had ever seen a female before.

She was, in her own way, exceptionally beautiful. And the coldness in her eyes was terrifying.

A stranger, with immense power... Broc didn't believe in prophecies and such, but it almost fit too beautifully.

"There's your intruder," Broc remarked, and gestured down at the mermaid. "Seems like the Elders might have been onto something will all their talk of prophecies."

Teaq didn't say a word.

The two of them watched as the guards tried to wrangle her up the slippery granite steps toward where the remaining soldiers were waiting. The Mermaid did not fight, but she did take a moment to spit on one of her captor's faces.

The latter cursed as he wiped his affected eye, then grabbed her by the throat.

"Don't lay a hand on me, wolf!" she hissed.

Broc raised an eyebrow. The guard hadn't transformed. How did she know about his inner beast?

The other soldier helped keep her contained. Meanwhile, Broc was mesmerized.

She wasn't as tall as most islanders, but the confidence and control with which she moved suggested that she was strong for her size. One thing was certain though; she acted entirely fearless. The predicament she was in— captured by her people's fiercest enemy—did not seem to faze her at all.

Sea Folk invaders had shown the same confidence in battle.

The enemy certainly knew how to make an impression. The entire incident was greatly worrying.

Perhaps her arrival was just the start of something much more ominous. After all, the Elders with their scriptures and prophecies had been on the lookout for the first sign of the upcoming age of war.

This was likely it.

Still, they couldn't very well let her go and wish this incident away. This was Black Isle territory. Intruders had to be punished. And she had been lurking around their defenses after all. They had to assume she was a spy.

"Lock her up underneath the deck so she doesn't dry out, then transfer her to a nice, cozy puddle in the castle dungeons at the earliest," Broc ordered.

He glanced at his brother, who was still frozen in place. What had gotten into him?

Teaq wasn't one to be easily startled, but this unexpected capture had clearly shaken him up. Was it the prospect of war that had him worried? This wasn't the Teaq Broc had grown up with.

"Brother?" Broc urged. "Will you accompany the prisoner transport?"

Teaq glanced to his side. His expression was even more serious than usual.

"Dark days are upon us."

Broc nodded. Once the Sea Folk found one of their own missing, especially one who had been on a mission to spy on Black Isle's fortifications, they would retaliate.

Teaq followed the procession of soldiers as they led the mermaid to the longship they had arrived on earlier. Broc remained on the sea wall and stared darkly over the choppy waters ahead.

He needed the Elders' help, and quickly. They simply did not have enough soldiers to man all the fortifications. One could never predict where an attack would land.

Black Isle's army consisted of extremely well trained, skilled fighters. He had bears and wolves manning his land defenses, and eagles in the skies above, each fully in control of their human as well as their animal form.

And for all his arrogance, Teaq was an excellent commander and strategist as well.

But the Sea Folk were a formidable enemy. Previous battles had not ended in victory for anyone.

Both sides had simply kept going until they had exhausted themselves.

So many lives lost.

This time, Broc had an added concern. Kelly. An innocent; a newcomer to all of it. The urge to keep her safe seemed all important.

Black Isle would need a lot more than just skill to win this war once and for all.

They needed a true advantage.

Broc once again thought of the prophecy. A stranger with great power, that could win or lose battles. The outcome of the war was not yet decided. The mermaid had shown no great interest in any of them. Put perhaps whatever her power was, it could be utilized somehow.

Perhaps the Elders would learn something from her that could tip the scales in their favor.

"Halt!" Broc called after the soldiers, who had nearly reached the dock. "I'm traveling with you."

———————◆———————

Broc paced the Great Hall. Back and forth, then back again. He'd wanted to call a meeting with all his advisors to discuss the mermaid's capture, but upon arriving at the castle found that Rhea had something even more pressing to discuss.

In a day, everything had changed. Only hours ago, he had known so clearly what to do. He'd had a definite plan for how things would go with Kelly. It had all been so simple, and now this.

"I don't understand. Are you absolutely certain that's what you saw, Rhea?" he demanded.

Rhea cocked her head to the side. "I would never lie to you, my king. She's a witch."

He shook his head. She had disapproved of Kelly since her arrival, for obvious reasons. But he did not believe her capable of such deceit. Rhea had always taken her role in his court seriously.

She'd always been honest, sometimes a little too honest, especially when she disagreed with him.

"It's really quite obvious that the prophecy is being fulfilled," Teaq remarked. "We can only hope it's not too late to counter this attack!"

Broc glared at him. *Oh he would just love to be right, wouldn't he.* This was the most Teaq had said since they'd left the Eastern Isle.

"This certainly demands further investigation. So we can determine what exactly has happened," Broc said. "And in case you've forgotten, we've just witnessed another incident that could very well be a part of this prophecy of yours."

Teaq's face twisted in anger. He had been unusually

quiet on the way back to the castle, and now he still seemed touchy at any mention of the mermaid.

"It's quite clear what has happened, brother!" Teaq argued. "The witch felt cornered, out there doing combat training with Rhea, and she exposed herself for what she is. An infiltrator. An enemy disguised as an innocent peasant girl from West Hythe. How the humans managed to find a witch after all these years, I cannot say. But she's here, so the hows and whys of it are irrelevant. This Reaping was obviously a trap."

"Now, now… " Broc interjected. "We do not know for sure what the humans intended. Or if they even knew about this. After all, the prophecy speaks of a *secret* power. Perhaps it was a secret to them as well."

Teaq and Rhea shared a dark look. The latter scoffed and shook her head.

"Fine, even if it was all *her* idea and *her* plan," Rhea began. "And the humans had no knowledge of it. We are still at the brink of war. The prophecy—"

Broc lost his calm at that point and stopped at the nearest table, banging his first hard onto its surface.

"I am fed up of everyone's speculations! Sick of it! We *are* at the brink of war, but with the Sea Folk, not with the humans. We'll get to the bottom of this matter with Kelly also, of course. I will speak with her. I must—"

"You will do nothing of the sort!" Teaq's heavy voice echoed against the granite clad walls of the Great Hall.

Broc squared up against him and kept his gaze locked firmly onto Teaq.

"In case you have forgotten. I am King. I do not need your permission to—"

"My king, if you'll hear us out…" Rhea interrupted.

Broc shook his head. No, he would not hear them out.

This was a dark day. Black Isle had gained two prisoners tonight, and potentially lost a queen. It was senseless.

Whose capture would more likely drag them into an armed conflict? An alleged witch, completely isolated from any of the people she grew up with? Or a mermaid, found lurking around the least defended island in their kingdom? Who was more likely to be a spy?

"We do not know for sure if Kelly means us any harm. But we are *certain* that the Sea Folk are our most pressing enemy. Am I wrong?"

Broc looked around for confirmation, but found Teaq merely staring in the distance, and Rhea sulking with her arms crossed in front of her chest.

His logical conclusion did not fit into their narrative. Too bad. He had always aimed to be a just ruler, but he was still king. It was his decision.

"I am going to interrogate our human prisoner now. Personally."

Rhea raised an arm. "My king, I do not think it safe for you to see her unguarded. We do not know enough of her powers."

"That's enough! She's chained up. She even let you carry her down the hillside without attempting to fight back or escape. What is she going to do to me? Blind me with a flash of light?" Broc bellowed.

Teaq shook his head and turned to leave without a word.

"Brother," Broc called after him. "Perhaps you could interrogate the other prisoner. Find out what she knows and whom she's told. And for all our sakes, try to find out if her people are planning an attack."

Rhea scoffed again. "She's not going to just spill everything."

Broc gestured vaguely. "Use your powers of persuasion, brother. Our safety may depend on it."

Teaq, who had paused for just a moment to hear Broc's orders, glanced back once, then started to walk away again without so much as a word of acknowledgement.

"My king," Rhea spoke up again.

Broc shook his head. "No. I've made my decision."

That was that. He also left the Great Hall and headed straight for the dungeons.

CHAPTER THIRTEEN

———◆———

"**W**ake up, my child," a voice spoke.

Kelly's eyes were still heavy, but she finally managed to open them. Standing over her was a figure, bathed in white light. It took a moment for her sight to adjust. Kelly tried to stir, but her body was so cold, her muscles refused to cooperate.

That face. That voice. Was she still imagining things?

"Mother," Kelly said. "Is that really you?"

The woman smiled. "Of course. I've been watching all this time."

"Watching and speaking to me."

Mother nodded. "Once you were ready to hear me. You called out for me and I came."

"How can it be? You're dead. I saw them bury your body all those years ago," Kelly whispered.

"Our people do not die as humans do. Our energy lingers in this realm."

Kelly shook her head. *What energy?* "I do not understand."

"You have questions. It is only natural."

Kelly finally managed to get up and approached the figure. But upon raising out her hand attempting to touch her, there was nothing there but air. Kelly looked down and found that her wrist was cuffed; a heavy chain connected it to a ring on the wall.

"How do I know you are real?" Kelly wondered aloud, as she rubbed her sore arms. As soon as she'd moved, all the aches she'd developed in training with Rhea had flared up again.

Mother let out a short laugh. "You know it in your heart."

Did she, though? Kelly wasn't so sure, but she kept her doubts to herself. Her wrist, meanwhile, was on fire. She tried to soothe it by massaging herself. The cuff made it impossible to reach the right spot.

Dejected, she wrapped herself in her woolen cloak and sat down again, resting her back against the stone wall.

"What do you mean 'our people'?" Kelly asked finally.

"Beings of light. Guardians of men."

Kelly frowned. Of course she'd heard of them, but those were just stories. Fairy tales.

"Witches and wizards," Kelly said.

Mother smiled mysteriously.

"What you're saying is you, my mother, are a witch. That's why you didn't truly die all those years ago?" Kelly wasn't sure what she expected the answer to be. Part of her suspected she might soon wake up and find this was all a strange dream. If only the pain wasn't so intense. You weren't supposed to feel pain in your sleep, right?

"You're focusing on the wrong thing, my child."

Kelly took a deep breath in an attempt to collect

herself. It all felt so real. But then, so had the events on the plateau earlier. And none of that could be real either. The lines between truth and fantasy were blurring and she could no longer tell one from the other.

She rubbed her eyes, and upon opening them again found that her mother was still very much there. If it was indeed her mother, and not some apparition pretending to be her.

"Come on. Think it through," Mother said.

Kelly pressed her lips together and tried to focus. Her mind was still so fuzzy. She averted her gaze.

Wait…

Her own hands had taken on a similarly eerie glow, though it was weak in comparison. Kelly's heart skipped a beat.

"You're saying… Oh, Mother, when you said 'our kind' you meant me as well?" She held up her right hand to have a better look. It was flickering, like a candle about to be extinguished, but it was unmistakable. She hadn't imagined it.

Mother smiled and nodded. "You're my blood. You and Ferris."

"I'm a… By God, that can't be true!" Her heart was pounding now. And with it, so was the throbbing pain in her right wrist.

"You saw it. The power we wield." Mother raised her hand, palm upwards. In the center of it, a small ball of blue light developed. Just as quickly as it had appeared, it vanished again.

"That's not… Rhea was tricking me."

Mother shook her head. "She provoked you. But there was no trickery involved."

"How come I never knew?"

"The world is a dangerous place for us. Even before the Great War, our kind was often misunderstood. We were persecuted. Over time, we were all but forgotten, except for the odd mention in ancient tales or songs. That was for the best."

"They'll punish me, Mother. Rhea said I'm an enemy of Black Isle. What do I do?" Kelly's voice cracked.

"She has her own troubles."

Kelly nodded. Her jealousy. She had disliked Kelly since her arrival because of it.

"Do not concern yourself with her. My child, you have to decide which side you're on."

"Side? I'm not on any side," Kelly protested.

Was she, though? Where did her loyalties lie? The villagers, including her father, who sent her off as a human sacrifice? She'd hated them for it. Her initial urge to escape had been equally about her own safety as it had been about revenge on the people who had singled her out all her life. The small-minded inhabitants of West Hythe, who had never made her feel like she belonged.

But now she was mostly indifferent about them.

"I don't side with the people of the mainland," Kelly

mumbled.

What of Black Isle and its people? They were a strange lot, and not all equally friendly. But here, everyone seemed to have a place. Everyone had value.

And up to this point, they had treated her fairly, all things considered.

And then there was Ferris. Only God knew where he was right now.

Mother smiled knowingly. "Think it through. When you find your answer, you'll know what to do."

Kelly looked around for the first time since waking. A cold, dark cell, only lit up by the glow surrounding her present company. The perfect place to put someone you want to forget.

Even if she decided, as Mother insisted she should. How would it help? She was stuck here.

Rhea had locked her up, and once word got out about what happened on the training ground today, everyone else would be equally keen to keep her here.

Witches were something to be feared. Something to be imprisoned and destroyed. *Misunderstood.*

Kelly should hate her for it; Rhea, the reason she was locked up. But she had found a new kind of clarity of mind in all of this confusion. Jealousy would make a person do things they ordinarily wouldn't. Bree had told her the other day that Rhea wasn't a bad person. And so far Kelly had no reason to doubt Bree's word.

And Broc... Why would Broc keep Rhea around; put

her in charge of the Castle Guard even, if she had no redeeming qualities?

Broc…

Did he even know she was down here? Did he condone it?

Kelly's heart grew heavier at the thought. She'd grown so close to him. He was her first. The only man she could imagine giving herself to.

She loved him, strange as it was.

Had he abandoned her down here as well? Cast her off once word of her sorcery reached him? Just the thought was enough to make her lose hope.

"What if it's no use? What if I'm stuck down here?"

Mother shook her head. "All this is only temporary. No chains can hold you. No cell can contain you."

Kelly frowned and looked down at her own hands again. The glow surrounding her skin had grown more intense and the flickering had stopped.

"Time will heal all."

Hopefully.

Kelly glanced up again. It had been a whirlwind of a day and this latest information was a lot to digest. She knew so little still, she didn't even know what to ask next.

Mother's own glow was weakening, though. *Strange.*

"You won't leave me again, will you?" Kelly wondered aloud.

Mother smiled. "I've passed a lot of my remaining

energy to you. I cannot stay like this for much longer. The spirit world is calling."

Kelly's chest tightened as she finally understood.

The light, Mother had transferred it to her. And the change was happening even faster now. She was weakening right before Kelly's eyes.

"No! I'm not ready! Don't leave me now when I need you the most!"

Mother shook her head. "My child. Now that you are self-aware, you'll find your own path."

Kelly's eyes burned with the onset of tears.

"I don't even know how to use this... This energy. I cannot do this alone."

"Oh, but you are not alone. You are of the light. We are one. Once you're ready, you'll know exactly what to do. Soon, you won't be able to see me anymore. But I'll always be in your heart."

Not only was the glow reducing quickly, it was as though Mother's form had become less defined. Her whole being was fading and taking on a translucent quality as she slowly turned away from Kelly.

"No, please!" Kelly begged. "At least tell me what powers we have?"

Mother looked back for a moment. "That's different for everyone. Yours seem to be defensive. It's all instinctive. You'll learn."

Kelly remembered being sucked out of her own body and watching the entire spectacle unfold. She had been able to hear Rhea's thoughts as well, it seemed.

By the time Kelly looked up to ask a follow-up question, she found that she was once again alone.

So much to think about. So much yet to learn. Mother's words still rang in her ears.

Choose a side.

The moment she'd stopped thinking about escaping, she'd made her choice. Her current predicament did not change that. But how would she convince everyone of her loyalties, especially Broc?

Even if she did by some miracle manage to prove herself, she was still a witch. And he was the king. Their love did not stand a chance.

Kelly curled up, burying her face in her hands. It was hopeless. He wouldn't be interested in hearing what she had to say.

She could only hope that sooner or later, when her powers grew, she would find a way out of this black hole. And then? She had no idea.

Minutes, hours went by, while she remained in the corner of her cold, dark cell. Giving up wasn't usually in her nature. But it was hard to remain hopeful when the only person in the whole world who understood you had just vanished into thin air.

Kelly let the entire conversation with Mother run through her mind again and again. She also thought about the events leading up to her incarceration.

She was a witch. It was so obvious now, even though she'd had trouble believing it at first.

When Rhea aimed to strike, Mother had granted her the energy for some kind of protective spell.

But as much as that explained, one thing was still a mystery. If she had defensive and mind reading powers, then why had Rhea's appearance changed, if only for a second?

Did she also have the ability to change people into animals? That seemed like an odd power to have.

Although her mind tried to wander back to Broc and the hopelessness of it all, she forced her thoughts away again and again.

Through the tears, loneliness and despair, she kept on focusing on this one problem: how Rhea had nearly turned into a bear.

Yet she was unable to solve it.

CHAPTER FOURTEEN

B roc was still shaking his head to himself when he neared the stone steps leading down into the bowels of the castle. But before he could enter the dungeon, he was intercepted.

"My king," a soft voice spoke.

Bree appeared from the shadows.

How had she found him here? Had she followed him from the Great Hall?

"Yes, Bree."

"I did as you asked," she said, while suspiciously scanning the hallway behind the two of them. "I followed Kelly today. Saw everything."

Broc, who had always banked on his calm and collected demeanor, grew tense. He hoped... he wasn't even sure what he was hoping for.

"Well, what did you see exactly?" Broc demanded, then immediately regretted his tone when

Bree flinched.

"It happened as Rhea said. Mostly." Bree kept her eyes fixed on the ground between them.

The girl was probably just nervous, but Broc felt his impatience at her vague responses grow. This time, he managed to collect himself.

"Mostly?" he asked.

"It was Rhea who instigated it. The battle training was rough. Rhea had an unfair advantage. Upon disarming Kelly, she…" Bree's voice trailed off and she scanned the hallway again.

"I would have intervened. I probably should have done so sooner," she muttered to herself.

"Go on, speak freely!" Broc urged.

"Rhea raised her sword, as if she meant to strike Kelly. Only, she didn't get the chance. A blue light surrounded the two of them and Rhea was thrown over the edge of the plateau."

Broc inhaled sharply. He didn't know what to make of it all. If Kelly indeed had magical powers… She had played the part of defenseless human very well indeed.

She'd tricked him.

And Rhea, she'd sensed it somehow. Even Teaq had had his suspicions.

A sense of dread filled his chest. He'd let her beauty enchant him.

"Thank you for bringing this to my attention," Broc spoke in a curt tone.

Was there any point in going down there anymore? He did still need to get to the bottom of it all, or he wouldn't find any rest.

"That's not all, my king," Bree said.

Broc turned to face the timid servant girl again.

"I've been watching her since. Taking care not to be seen by anyone, including Kelly herself."

"And?"

"I don't think she had any idea what was happening. On the way down the hill she passed out, and when she awoke, I heard her talking to someone. So I peered inside her cell. There was a mysterious figure in there with her. She kept calling her 'Mother'."

Broc frowned. Perhaps Kelly was talking in her sleep, just like she had done that morning, before any of this had happened. Still, his curiosity was sparked.

"But surely, there was no one inside with her?" Broc asked.

Bree pressed her lips together. Her face was full of doubt, and healthy dose of fear.

"By all means, girl. Speak!"

"Oh, but there was someone in her cell. A woman. I've no idea how she could have got in. The guard never left the hallway. I only managed to pass him because I'd changed to my animal form."

Broc was stunned for a moment.

"She was…" Bree finally did look terrified. "She was glowing! It lit up the whole cell."

"So what? You said she'd done that even out on the plateau," Broc mumbled.

"Not Kelly! Her mother. The strange woman was glowing."

That made even less sense.

"So you're saying we have two witches locked up down

below?"

Bree shook her head. "No, that's the thing, the woman vanished into thin air when their conversation was finished. Like she'd never even been there at all. That's what I can't comprehend. How is that even possible?"

The girl was rambling. Understandably, she was deeply affected by everything she had witnessed. Still, Broc had to know the whole story. There was so much he did not yet understand.

"Back to Kelly. You said she didn't know what was happening? What makes you say that?" Broc asked.

"Just, their conversation. Kelly thought Rhea had tricked her and that's why she was imprisoned. I don't think she realized she had powers. Until that woman, her so-called mother, told her about it."

"Ah." Broc scratched his beard.

A glimmer of hope after the darkest of hours. Was it possible that Kelly, his intended, was innocent after all?

Sure, she was still a witch. But if there was no *intent* there…

"Thank you, Bree. Your loyalty will be rewarded."

Bree nodded briefly. "Thank you, my king."

Broc watched her leave in a hurry. Then he quickly continued on his way to the dungeons.

Somewhere in this maze of dark corridors, further down below the mountain, the other prisoner was being held.

Broc did not care to look for her, or to check if Teaq

had indeed followed his orders and started interrogating her. He only had one goal: to speak with Kelly.

Throughout this entire debacle, he'd done his best to remain objective. He'd tried to listen to Rhea's story, and act statesmanlike and fair. But there was a large part of him that was incapable of rational thinking when it came to Kelly.

His inner beast had already chosen her. Claimed her. How could he deny that?

He had to find a way out of this mess. Luckily, what Bree had told him gave him something to cling onto.

"My king!" The guard posted near Kelly's cell jumped to attention.

Broc gestured at him to calm down. "I mean to speak with the prisoner."

He held out his hand, and waited. It took the guard a moment, before he realized Broc wanted the bundle of keys and indeed handed it over.

"Shall I…" He didn't finish his question. The man was obviously new at his job and uncertain about himself. He'd chosen to stand as far away from Kelly's cell as he could manage. No wonder Bree had slipped past easily and watched Kelly unseen.

"You're excused. I will do this alone," Broc said.

The guard hesitated, but then shrugged and left as ordered. Rhea and Teaq had a lot of leeway in how they acted around Broc, but most of the soldiers on this island did not have that luxury. An order was an order, especially when it came directly from the highest of places.

Broc's heart was racing in a way he hadn't felt in a very long time. Faced with the prospect of speaking to Kelly at last made him feel exposed. She held a strange power over him.

Magic?

Probably not, even though Rhea might have wanted to believe so.

Not that it mattered, what Rhea believed. He closed his eyes and focused.

Kelly was just beyond that heavy door. He could hear her heartbeat. Her breaths.

That sweet scent of hers that had enchanted him right from the start tried to draw him nearer even now.

His inner beast reacted almost violently. He had to get inside there. To find out if she was still loyal to him.

If their bond was still true.

He rushed to open the door. It swung wide, with a violent screech. Kelly, who had been lying on the cold floor, flinched backwards in fear.

"Don't be afraid," Broc said, as he stepped in and closed the door behind him. For the conversation he was intending to have, it was best that nobody, especially the novice guard, overheard.

Her perfume overwhelmed her; tore at his insides. He found it near impossible to control himself and not rush over there to comfort her. She'd obviously been miserable;

who wouldn't be, locked up in this cold, damp place. There were no windows; no source of fresh air or light. It was easy to forget all sense of time in here.

It was a terrible injustice to find his intended here, especially if everything Bree had told him was true.

What happened today?

He wanted to know every detail, but he could not bring himself to ask. Every question that entered his mind sounded like an accusation.

"It seems I haven't been honest with you," Kelly whispered.

She looked so small, so vulnerable.

"It seems not," he said.

His voice sounded a lot weaker than he had intended. Such was his relief that she'd spoken first.

"I hope you'll believe me. I don't even fully understand myself what happened out there."

Kelly looked up with those big green eyes of hers. "I'm a witch. This I've learned to be true. But I mean you or your people no harm."

Even though her face and hands were muddy, and her hair tangled and dull, her beauty was still blinding. Those large, red-rimmed eyes... She'd been crying; the dirt on her cheeks was streaked.

Broc was no stranger to physical pain. Nearly everyone on these islands had seen battle at some point or other. To be a warrior of Black Isle meant to be scarred by combat.

But seeing *her* like this was unbearable. It all but tore him in half.

During the few days they had spent together, a connection had formed. A sacred bond between lovers that many a song had been written about. He'd never taken the stories seriously, but now he knew better.

Fate had brought them together.

Their bond was true. How could he deny it now?

"I believe you," he whispered.

Kelly's eyes widened in surprise.

All the doubts that had plagued him since he'd heard the news were gone now that he saw the truth in her face.

But that didn't mean that this matter was resolved. There were still Rhea and Teaq, and a council of Elders that would need convincing

As king, his decision was final in most matters, but pardoning a supposedly dangerous enemy after wounding one of their own, that would go too far. It would open him up to challenge, something which Teaq would be all too happy to take advantage of.

But to have their union broken and their love destroyed by an unjust accusation, that was even worse.

"Choose a side," Kelly mumbled.

"What?" Broc asked.

She shook her head. "Just what someone told me. To choose a side and everything would work itself out."

"Your mother," Broc stated.

Kelly looked up again. "How did you know?"

"Bree. I'd sent her to watch over you. She overheard." Broc had answered mindlessly, without considering the consequences. But it was too late to take it back.

"Bree was *here?*" Kelly asked.

There it was. The inevitable question. Answering her truthfully meant ignoring his promise to Teaq and the others. It would mean exposing Black Isle's secret to a supposed enemy.

Broc nodded.

"I never saw her," Kelly stammered.

"Some of us, we can move almost unseen," Broc said.

Kelly frowned, then closed her eyes and remained perfectly still. A soft glow surrounded her only briefly.

Broc's heart raced as he watched a change overcome her. Her expression became vacant, her body looked almost lifeless.

Show yourself, her voice entered his mind. Then he felt the change in himself. His inner beast, which had been raging to get out ever since he smelled her presence, answered her call and clawed his way to the surface.

It only took the briefest of moments before Broc managed to force him back in.

Kelly gasped in surprise.

"What did I just see?" she stammered.

Broc wasn't sure how to respond. He wasn't quite sure what had happened himself.

"You're…" Kelly stood up and took a hesitant step in his direction. "You're like Rhea? Half bear half man!"

That was impossible. Rhea was always in control of those primal impulses. Had she shown her true self to Kelly in the heat of the moment?

And if she had just seen Broc's inner bear, how come she wasn't terrified like most humans were after their first sighting?

"I… What did you just do?" Broc asked.

Kelly paused. "I'm not entirely sure. When I focus really hard, it seems I can enter people's minds."

Seeing as he'd heard her thoughts too, even if just for a moment, perhaps that wasn't all she could do.

He walked over to her and took her hands. Cold as ice. Seeing the shackles on her wrists filled him with rage as well as regret. He had to get her out of here, and soon.

All he needed was a way to justify it to the others. So that they wouldn't call his judgement into question and challenge his right to the throne.

This power of hers, though she seemed to not have it fully under control, brought with it great opportunity.

"This is how we will convince them," Broc said.

Kelly frowned and shook her head. "I don't understand."

"The Elders. Teaq and Rhea. You'll practice this skill of yours, and we'll use it to our advantage."

"I can try." Kelly looked up at him with large, hesitant eyes.

"Let's get you out of here first," Broc said. "Nobody else knows about what went on today. There's no sense in missing the third night of the feast and raising suspicions where there shouldn't be any."

"You mean to do this tonight?"

He gently rubbed her icy hands between his. "I can't leave you here. But perhaps it's best if we keep you in hiding for a few days before confronting everyone."

A tear formed in the corner of Kelly's eye as she smiled up at him.

Thank you. Her voice entered his mind. *Thank you for believing in me.*

Kelly looked down at her wrists. A blue light enveloped the restraints until they snapped open and fell to the ground.

It should have shocked him, perhaps even frightened him. But watching Kelly's magic, however small, just filled Broc with pride.

"She was right, my mother," Kelly said. "She said I'd know what to do. Once the time came and I'd made my choice."

"And, what have you decided?" Broc asked.

"That I'm on your side. For as long as you'll have me."

CHAPTER FIFTEEN

———————— ◆ ————————

Kelly closed her eyes and inhaled deeply. She was so grateful.

For her mother, who had saved her from Rhea's blinding jealousy, even if her well-meaning intervention had created a whole host of other issues.

And Broc, for believing her when she wasn't even fully sure what to believe herself.

She was also grateful for this hot bath Bree had run for her in preparation for tonight. Despite the two days' rest since being rescued from the dungeon, her body was still bruised and sore.

Their reunion was awkward at first, but Bree quickly relaxed once Kelly confided in her about everything that had happened down in the dungeon.

It was such a relief to have another person to talk to.

Her release had been handled quietly. Rhea and Teaq had not been informed. The only people who knew so far were Broc, obviously, Bree, and the guard outside her cell. Thankfully nobody else had thought to check her chambers, so their secret was still safe.

She'd spent these days in hiding, trying to hone her skills by practicing on either Broc or Bree. But tonight was the night Kelly would reveal herself.

She would attend the final night of the Reaping feast.

The element of surprise would be on their side. Then she'd use her newfound powers to appease everyone.

She'd have to confront Broc's council of advisors, starting with Rhea and Teaq. Just how easily she would be able to convince them to see her not as a treacherous enemy to their way of life, but an innocent bystander in all of this, was hard to say.

There was no conspiracy here. She hadn't been put up as an offering in the Reaping to infiltrate their ranks and destroy them from within. What a ridiculous notion. The villagers of West Hythe were way too set in their ways to come up with such a cunning plan.

A woman spy. Most, her own father included, would spit on the idea.

The mainland was a very different place from the Black Isles. Surely everyone would see that eventually?

Kelly's stomach growled angrily. She hadn't eaten for hours. But until she could change everyone's minds and secure her place here, food was the last thing on her mind.

"Bree," Kelly called out. "If you could hand me that towel… I'd better get ready now."

———◆———

When Kelly entered the Great Hall, accompanied by Bree, she was once again painfully aware of the eyes fixated on her. Two pairs, in particular.

Teaq and Rhea could not hide their shock at her

presence and jumped up from their seats in protest. It was unnerving to watch their faces twist and morph to reveal their true selves; half bear for Rhea, and Teaq was half wolf.

"My king!" Teaq's voice was so loud, Kelly could hear it over the chatter and commotion created by the ongoing celebrations. "We must talk, immediately!"

Broc gestured at him to sit back down, but it had no effect.

Rhea was even more distraught. Her face reddened with anger.

"This is… My God, this is an insult!"

Some of the other giants looked up, curious at what had sparked her outburst. Their faces also changed briefly, enabling Kelly to finally see the full diversity on the island. Bears and wolves, she'd already known about. Now she also saw foxes, badgers, as well as the occasional eagle.

Oh no. Would they be able to tell now that she was different? That her influence had revealed their secret?

Kelly's heart was pounding.

This was never going to be easy, but Kelly hadn't counted on being put on trial in front of the entire populace of the castle. Her skills were still in their infancy. How would she manage, if she continued to feel so… *watched?*

Broc intervened quickly. "This is not the time or place. We're feasting. Celebrating our survival as a people."

Rhea looked furious as she stared Kelly down. Flared

nostrils, lips curled slightly into a snarl.

Luckily it seemed the rest of the crowd was losing interest and focused once more on the filled plates in front of them. Kelly could breathe a little easier again.

Time to focus. She had one chance to make this right. She could not afford any mistakes now.

Just like she had done with Broc multiple times already, she closed her eyes and concentrated. Like a muscle undergoing regular training, slipping in and out of her own body had become easier with each attempt. She started to float above the crowd unseen, allowing her to look down on her own form as well as Bree, who continued to stand by her side.

Then she diverted her attention to Rhea.

Our king has been compromised. This witch is going to be the end of us all!

Kelly focused again and allowed her thoughts to connect more deeply with Rhea.

Just as she'd done with Broc, earlier, and even Bree, in an attempt to explain herself, she opened her mind. Her thoughts, memories, hopes and dreams. Everything flowed freely. In return, Kelly felt the envy, the hate Rhea had shown her as well as the hopes she'd had for her future.

He was mine. I ought to become queen, not you. The rules be damned.

Kelly responded. *I understand your sorrow. I mean you no harm.*

Rhea's expression softened as she sank back into her seat. Stunned and speechless.

But... you're a witch.

That I am. But I'm not your enemy. She transferred her own emotions, her own memories into Rhea's mind as best she could. Broc had likened their previous connections to a dream. Fragmented at times, but so very real.

Rhea shook her head; her expression was ashen. Their exchange had taken its toll.

Kelly's energy was waning as well, but she knew she had to make a final push.

Teaq.

The general was a difficult case. His mind was a lot more challenging and guarded than Rhea's had been.

Kelly found it hard to penetrate him.

I mean you no harm. Let me in.

He didn't react immediately. His walls were thick and his defenses strong.

When she finally reached him, what she found surprised her. Beyond his harsh exterior, he wasn't hateful or even angry. He wasn't even thinking about Kelly so much as he was preoccupied with someone else.

His thoughts were a confused mass of regret and guilt. Being inside of his thoughts filled Kelly's heart with dread. He knew something he wasn't sharing. Dangerous secrets. Kelly wasn't sure she wanted to know. Teaq was a very troubled man.

Overcome by a guilt no man should have to bear.

She fought through her own tears as she once again tried to share her truth with him.

He wasn't open to her. It was no use.

Kelly's body demanded her return. She had used up all the energy she had. As she entered her own self again, she wasn't quite the same. That sense of dread she'd picked up in Teaq's mind had lodged itself in her heart. Looking at him now, she couldn't hide her sadness.

He did not speak a word as he turned away from the festivities and walked away in silence. A hollow man. With unspeakable secrets even Kelly's growing powers could not decipher.

"We will discuss everything, in time," Broc spoke up again. "But tonight, we celebrate. Our people deserve it. Who knows how long this peace will last."

Rhea nodded; she didn't look happy about it, but she no longer had the will to fight.

"Where's he going," Broc wondered aloud, as he watched Teaq leave the Great Hall.

Kelly shook her head. "I don't know. Your brother… he has a troubled soul."

Broc gave her a questioning look, but she just shook her head instead of answering. The darkness within him had shaken her to her core. Best not to dwell on it now.

They had overcome the first hurdle toward redemption.

Tonight, they would celebrate this initial victory. Later, they would deal with the Elders the same way.

———◆———

They hadn't stayed until the end of the feast.

Beyond the obligatory speech by Broc, and the food Kelly's body so desperately needed, there wasn't much keeping them there. They walked through the long, dark corridors in silence, until they reached the Watch Point.

"It's funny," Kelly spoke up, making her voice just a little louder than the winds whistling around the castle fortifications.

"What is?"

"Just how quickly things change."

Broc nodded then stared darkly at the waters below. It would be so easy to connect with him and find out what he was thinking, but it did not seem fair.

Kelly wrapped herself tighter in her woolen cloak; still the gales tried their best to penetrate the heavy fabric.

"I never liked this tradition, you know," Broc said.

Kelly looked up at him, studying his face. Hardened by the difficult life on these islands, yet also kind.

"The Reaping. It's a necessary evil," Broc elaborated.

"I've wondered about that."

Broc looked down at her and smiled briefly.

"Of course you have." His expression became serious again. "Towards the end of the Great War, our numbers had declined so much it would have been impossible to continue on without outside help. Sisters bearing their brothers' children… It's a recipe for disaster."

"Hence the treaty," Kelly whispered. She'd known as much since the first night of the Feast.

"Yes. But despite the feasting and the celebrations, we don't revel in it. Taking someone away from their family… Their way of life. I don't take it lightly."

Kelly also turned thoughtful as she looked ahead at the dark clouds collecting overhead. "In a way, it's almost a kindness. The mainland is not always a pleasant place for women."

Broc took her hand. Excitement washed over her as it did each time he touched her, though this time the feeling was bittersweet. The heaviness she'd carried with her since infiltrating Teaq's mind had never fully left.

"Dark days are ahead. We're expecting war. Bringing you into this as an innocent, it's not just."

"I already told you, I've made my choice. I don't have anywhere else I'd rather be," Kelly said.

"I still have to ask."

Broc took her other hand as well and got down on one knee in front of her. The sight of this powerful man in a pose of submission took Kelly's breath away.

"Knowing of all the uncertainty and danger ahead, would you still become my queen? The mother of my children?" Broc's voice was almost a whisper.

His concern for her almost broke her heart. To think of how she'd arrived here. How she really hadn't had much of a choice. All that had changed when she found out about her powers. Now she had nothing but choices. And none made more sense than this one.

"Yes. Of course. Always."

"I will protect you. I will try to keep you safe if it's the last thing I do. But this life is not without dangers."

Kelly freed her hands from his grasp and wrapped her arms around his neck, which for a change was conveniently within her reach. She buried her face into his hair and closed her eyes. Even though she wasn't trying to, she could feel his emotions deep within her own heart.

"In barely a week I've learned more about life, and love, than all the years that came before. Suddenly I feel like I don't need much protection after all."

Broc pulled back just enough to look at her. "The prophecy."

"What?"

"The Elders spoke of an outsider whose powers could win or lose wars."

"They meant me?" Kelly didn't need an answer. It made perfect sense. Her defensive powers could be helpful. If only she could develop them further.

Broc gathered Kelly up in his arms and stood up again. Kelly rested her head against his shoulder as he carried her back inside the castle.

She would train. She would do everything she could to

help. Just not tonight.

Tonight they'd celebrate their love. Just as they had done on prior nights. Only this time, there were no more secrets between them. Were there?

She inhaled deeply, closing her eyes again as his masculine scent threatened to overwhelm her. How had he done it? How had he awakened such fire within her, that only his touch could douse?

Magic…

"Do we *have* to wait until marriage?" Kelly wondered aloud.

Broc chuckled as he continued to carry her through the maze of stone hallways, leading inevitably to his quarters. "It *is* tradition."

She knew he was right, of course, prompting her to change course.

"Then how about…" she paused for a moment, uncertain if she should complete her thought.

"What is it, my darling?"

"You show me your true self. Willingly." Kelly's heart started to race. The suggestion had escaped her lips before she could fully think it through.

"I thought… You'd already seen?" Broc asked, taking a step back.

"Yes… Maybe… I can't shake the idea that there's more to it." Kelly waited with bated breath. Had she gone too far? Had she offended him?

Finally, a smile broke through his previously thoughtful expression. "I don't see the harm."

They rushed the rest of the way to Broc's quarters, just as they'd done the previous night. Once he'd secured the door behind them, he cast off his garments, one by one, revealing more of his tan skin.

It was hard to see in the flicker of the torch on the wall, but Kelly found herself once again marveling at the beauty that was him. She'd never seen a man quite like Broc before.

Then again, he *wasn't* like any ordinary man, was he?

He closed his eyes, his face tense with concentration, then within the blink of an eye, a change came over his entire body. Muscle, morphing and twisting into alien shapes. Fur sprouting where there had been none.

Kelly covered her hand with her mouth, though an errant gasp escaped when the transformation was complete.

It wasn't just his face, like before. Within a fraction of a second, the giant man who had just stood before her had turned into a real life bear. Claws, teeth, snout and all.

Then within the blink of an eye, the animal was gone, and Broc was himself again.

"Are you alright?" he asked.

Kelly was speechless. Her heart was still racing.

"I hope I did not scare you?" Broc urged.

She shook her head. "No… No, that was simply…"

"Terrifying?"

"I was going to say, magnificent." She smiled and let out a nervous giggle. "None of what I'd seen earlier could have prepared me for this."

She dropped back onto the bed and breathed deeply. Her man. Her future husband. He was something quite special indeed.

EPILOGUE

———◆———

How far she had come.

Kelly looked at her reflection in the mirror that had finally arrived for her only this morning. The white dress with gold embroidery wasn't just elegant, it was fit for a queen.

"It's lovely," Bree remarked.

Kelly glanced at the young giant's form, also caught within the mirror, and couldn't suppress a smile.

When she'd first arrived here a couple of weeks ago, she couldn't even have imagined the reason why there wasn't a single reflective surface anywhere in the castle. Mirrors revealed the Black Islanders' animal form. Bree's feathered complexion smiled back at her.

An owl. How fitting.

Of course, at the time of her arrival, nobody, not even Kelly herself, could have predicted how things would turn out. That she'd develop the power to see everyone's inner animal without outside help. How hard they'd tried to keep their secret…

"Are you ready? It's almost time." Bree's question dragged Kelly out of her daydream.

"Yes, of course."

She made sure everything was in place, and readjusted the crown that sparkled from on top of her deep red curls.

Finally, she slipped into a pair of delicate shoes decorated with sparkly stones matching the embroidery on her dress. These people weren't the sort to dress up. But for today— for their new queen—they had gone all out.

It was time.

Kelly's heart was aflutter as she walked slowly and deliberately down the aisle. The Great Hall, elaborately decorated for the occasion, was filled with so many onlookers, there was only a narrow space between them for Kelly to pass. Even those who normally did not reside on the main island had made the trip to see their new queen.

Broc waited at the end, together with the leader of the Elders; a frail man in a long light grey cloak whom Kelly recognized from her meeting with the entire Council some weeks earlier. Uri.

Teaq and Rhea stood by further towards Broc's right. Neither were happy about it, but they'd finally accepted Broc's decision once it turned out that the Elders were onboard too. It was all part of the prophecy. She would use her powers to help them in their time of need. If it ever came to that.

Finally, Kelly stood in front of Broc. Her soon to be husband. Looking into his eyes still made her knees weak, but she tried not to show it. Not in front of all these people.

Uri cleared his throat and slowly raised his right arm.

The crowd grew silent.

"This," he spoke with a thin and shaky voice. "Is a very special day. For today, we celebrate a royal union."

The crowd cheered, then settled again as Uri shot a strict look in their direction.

"It is in front of you all that Broc Bearclaw, King of the Black Isles and ruler of the Northern Sea, accepts as his queen Kelly Chaslain of West Hythe. May their bond remain true forever, and their union fruitful!"

Uri shuffled backward as the crowd erupted again.

Broc took his place in front of Kelly. In his hands was a heavily decorated sheath and sword. It was the most beautiful weapon she had ever seen. Intricately carved designs decorated the shiny metal. The handle was studded with expertly cut precious stones in a multitude of colors. With one palm underneath the handle and the other underneath the sheath, he got down on one knee and held it up in Kelly's direction.

They'd practiced this bit, the night before, but Kelly still felt her throat close up as he started to speak.

"This sword is a symbol of my protection. Accept it and know I and my people will keep you safe for as long as you shall live. As my queen. My wife. My life."

She did her best to swallow her emotions.

Kelly had never wished for marriage. On the mainland it was just this thing everyone did. Like being born and dying, all the girls of a certain age got married. It had nothing to do with love, or passion, as far as Kelly could tell.

But this…It was something else entirely. He'd asked her. She'd said yes. And now he was asking again in front of everyone in terms grander than even the most romantic poem or song.

She looked down at her man, who remained in position at her feet. At those honest eyes she had fallen for. The lips that seemed to beg for her kisses.

Kelly reached out and took the sword. It weighed heavy in her hands as she also supported it from either end with her palms.

"I accept," she whispered. "My king."

"Go on, kiss her already," someone at the back of the crowd shouted.

"Yeah!" More people joined in.

"Oh come on, don't ruin the moment now," Broc retorted, then looked up at her again.

Though her eyes had become a bit moist, she could not suppress a grin. These people… *Her people*, they were a strange lot. But their enthusiasm was contagious.

He got up, slowly, and waited as Kelly fumbled with the leather strap of the sword, fastening it around her waist.

Then he held out his hand, which Kelly gladly accepted.

"May I?" he mouthed.

She nodded.

Broc pulled her into his arms and kissed her, just as the crowd had demanded. Applause erupted. People whistled and shouted.

She ought to be embarrassed, but the excitement that swept over everyone had infected her too. She wrapped her own arms around him too, and forgot herself in the moment.

Music started to play; barrels of wine and beer appeared through the various doors of the Great Hall. The formalities had ended and the party had begun.

But neither Broc nor Kelly were interested in any of that. They stayed but for a moment. Once the well-wishers got distracted, and nobody came up to congratulate them anymore, they quietly slipped away. Free from further scrutiny, away from the well-meaning but crude remarks some of the giants had shouted their way. Nothing stood in their way anymore.

Today was the first day of the rest of their lives.

Man and wife.

King and Queen.

They paused in front of Broc's quarters, giving him the chance to carry her across the threshold. He'd done it before, many times, but it felt different now. There was no more tradition forbidding them from following their hearts. They did not have to hold back anymore. For the very first time, they could follow their desires to the very end.

"It's beautiful," Kelly whispered, as Broc lay her down

on top of his giant bed. In all the time she'd been here, the vegetation she'd taken for granted on the mainland had been sorely missing. But for tonight, Broc's bed had been carefully decorated with flower petals in various colors.

"You like it?" he asked.

It wasn't really a question, because Kelly was certain the way she stared into his eyes now was enough of an answer.

She inhaled deeply of the familiar scent of his room; the leather gear he was so fond of added a spicy tone to the sweet fragrance of the flowers.

The first blooms of early summer. A little part of the home she'd left behind.

Broc got off the bed, just for a moment, before settling on the end. He lifted the skirt of her wedding dress, exposing her shapely thighs and spreading them with both hands.

She had already become familiar with this strong, confident grip. Firm but not painful. A man on a mission she could not refuse.

He leaned down between her legs and tasted her flesh.

It wasn't new to her, and yet each time he worshipped her like this felt unique.

Kelly settled into the pillows and closed her eyes. She focused solely on this most exquisite pleasure which he bestowed upon her most intimate parts.

The tip of his tongue caressed her where it mattered

most, then before the sensation grew too intense, backed away again to give her some relief. Though the room was cool as usual, her skin was on fire. It was a burn only his touch could soothe.

She reached for his hair, gripping it firmly between her fingers.

This was otherworldly. This love they shared. This pleasure they could inspire in each other.

But it was only the beginning.

Kelly's hips bucked, her body aching for a firmer touch. Broc's lips responded.

Then suddenly, he backed away.

"No! Don't stop!" Kelly pleaded.

He smiled and licked his bottom lip as he looked down at her. His eyes were a deep black, yet still managed to simmer. He would not be denied what was his tonight.

Not that Kelly could ever refuse him. Her own desire was much too strong.

Was this how all the girls felt on their wedding night? So special.

She was the luckiest bride in the world.

"I want you. All of you," he whispered.

There was a rawness in his voice that spoke directly to Kelly's most inner urges. Whenever she was with him, a sweet ache developed in her lower abdomen that she could not put into words. Tonight, it had grown more intense than ever.

"You have me," she responded.

"You know what this means," he said.

Kelly shook her head. It was beautiful, insane, unexpected and entirely surreal. But that was all she knew.

"If we become one tonight…" Broc started.

"Yes?"

"Then perhaps, our family will grow."

Kelly bit her bottom lip. *Family*. It was hard not to think of Ferris and what had become of him upon hearing that word. And yet, it also filled her with hope, and excitement about what the future might hold.

"I'm ready."

Broc cast off his clothes. There he was at his most honest.

Glorious. Powerful. Naked.

As he approached, Kelly could see in more detail. His skin, marked by the scars he'd earned in training and battle alike. She traced them all, one by one, with the tip of her finger.

Across his chest, his arms, even his back. How much pain he must have endured over the years.

At the same time he lavished her shoulders and cleavage with kisses. She ought to feel weak and helpless in front of him. Instead, she felt powerful.

She raised herself off the bed, allowing him access to the laces at the back of her dress. Free at last.

His manhood stood proudly, almost teasing her with its presence. This wasn't something nice girls talked about, but Kelly knew what to do. The growing fire in her stomach burnt up any remaining trace of patience.

She ached for him.

She was ready and would no longer be denied this ultimate pleasure.

As her dress fell to the floor, she felt empowered to take this new step with him. She crawled back onto the bed, and reached for his chest, pushing him backward against the pillows. He did not protest.

Then she straddled his hard, muscular thighs and lowered herself down on top of him, supported by his strong grasp. A raw moan escaped her lips as she allowed him inside of her.

His body merged with hers for the very first time. It stung at first, but not in a bad way. Soon, the initial pain was forgotten.

This was the way to soothe the sweet ache within. She started to rock back and forth on top of him, guided by instinct as much as his hands. He reached for her neck, twirling his fingers around stray locks of her hair as she held on tightly to his wrist for balance.

Her other hand found its way down onto his abs.

Though she was on top, he was moving along with her. Where her movement ended, his began.

A perfect rhythm, like waves crashing onto the beach.

Many times she'd imagined what this would be like. Two becoming one.

She closed her eyes, swept up in the magic of the

moment.

Rolling her hips backwards and forwards, she felt her thoughts reach a new plane. Reality mattered no more. The threat Broc had mentioned so many times, the coming war.

It was irrelevant. As long as they had each other, everything would work itself out.

Faster and faster, they moved. Like a dance, only much more intimate.

Their bodies seemed to sense exactly what the other desired. A slight pause to build the tension, or a more feverish pace to try and relieve it.

The ache was growing. Ever sweeter, ever more intense.

She would not last through the night. The anticipation for this moment had been too great.

Kelly opened her eyes again, and found Broc already staring up at her. His face betrayed a change in him too. He wasn't his calm, collected self. He was no longer in control.

Their union had brought out his wild side.

He dug his fingers into her hips, spurring her on. She sped up, more and more, feverishly working towards their mutual release.

It was coming. She knew it.

And with it, she knew something else.

His prediction would come true. She could sense it.

As he reached the pinnacle of his pleasure, he let out a primal groan. A shudder originated in his body, seemingly transferring all his pleasure into her.

She could keep quiet no longer, crying out with tears in her eyes as she tensed up as well. Bearing down hard on top of his still trembling manhood, he exploded into her.

Kelly's mind filled with light. Her eyes, wide open.

Through the blinding white surrounding her, Broc's face appeared in front of her. His eyes, staring into hers.

"I love you, Kelly Chaslain of West Hythe."

"I love you too," Kelly whispered in response.

The words held less meaning than the feeling that passed unrestricted between the two.

Light.

Love.

Life.

Kelly snapped back into reality, and found that she was still where she had been only moments earlier. The blinding light had gone, replaced by the dimly lit room decorated with flowers. Underneath her on the bed, her man, with a satisfied smile on his face.

"What happened," he asked.

Kelly shook her head and returned his smile. "I don't know. A vision. A dream."

"And what did you learn in this vision?"

She reached down and placed his hand on her lower abdomen. It still took her breath away just how much bigger his hand was than hers.

"That you're right. That our family will grow."

He grinned widely. "Well, that's a good vision indeed."

He threaded his fingers through hers and pulled her down into his arms. She rested her head against his chest, but did not stir otherwise. Nothing else mattered anymore. Kelly was content to remain in this embrace, listening to the calming beat of his heart.

If she died right now, it would have been with a smile on her face.

That was how they remained. Time had lost all meaning. They were not in a rush to get up.

Until a distant sound disturbed the peace.

"What was that?" Kelly asked, lifting her head. The noise had sent a shiver down her naked skin.

Broc's expression and tone had grown dark in an instant.

"The war horn. As we've feared. It has begun."

- THE END -

Shifters of Black Isle continues with *The Soldier and the Siren*, coming in September 2018.

ABOUT THE AUTHOR

———◆———

Dear Reader,

Thanks for reading *Claimed by the King*. This is the first book in my brand new *Shifters of Black Isle* series, a collection of stories set in a fantasy world full of mystery, magic and fantastical creatures. I hope you're as excited as I am about the rest of the series as I am!

I may have only released my first book in 2015, but I'm not new to writing in general. In fact, my mom still tells me to this day about how I would make up stories, and attempt to record them in my clumsy, shaky handwriting from the moment I learned to read and write. From there I went on to write fan fiction and other stuff meant for my own eyes only.

I've always enjoyed stories of the fantastic and paranormal. Vampires, shape shifters, witches and magic, all featured in the books I loved the most, even when I was still growing up. But it wasn't until much later that I got into romance. One of the first writers (an independent author just like me!) I came across was Tina Folsom, via her Scanguards

Vampire series. I was hooked. From there I went on to read more paranormal romance until I found a new kind of hero I loved: bear shifters, like the kind written by Milly Taiden, Zoe Chant, and T.S. Joyce. What I love about bears is how they can be all strong and independent, a bit reclusive, and almost grumpy, but they always end up having a heart of gold (plus they tend to know their food, and we all know that a man who can cook is doubly sexy). All that (except for the shifting into a powerful bear) almost exactly describes the sort of man I ended up falling for and marrying in real life, so it's no surprise that this is what I started my publishing career with.

To find out more, check:

LoreleiMoone.com (And why not sign up for the newsletter to be the first to find out about new releases.)

You can also get in touch with me via Facebook (search for Lorelei Moone), or email at info@loreleimoone.com

x Lorelei

HAVE YOU MET THE SCOTTISH WEREBEARS?

————— ◆ —————

Before there was Alpha Squad, there were the Scottish Werebears... And if you sign up for Lorelei Moone's mailing list at loreleimoone.com, you get Book 1, Scottish Werebear: An Unexpected Affair absolutely free!

Titles in the Scottish Werebears series include:

An Unexpected Affair

A Dangerous Business

A Forbidden Love

A New Beginning

A Painful Dilemma

A Second Chance

These individual books in the Scottish Werebears series are best read in order. They can also be enjoyed as part of the Scottish Werebear: Complete Collection boxed set.

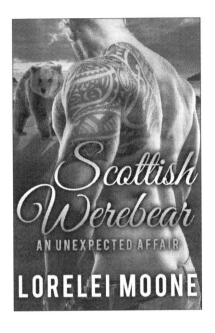

When romance novelist, Clarice Adler, hides herself away in a secluded holiday cottage to finish a book, the last thing she needs is another relationship. Imagine her surprise when she falls head over heels for the man who runs the place. Derek McMillan knows Clarice is his mate, but he's a bear shifter and she's human and the two simply don't mix. They are literally worlds apart; can they find a way to come together?

Get this book for free by joining Lorelei Moone's mailing list at loreleimoone.com!